Other

& DIFFERENT

Other & Different - First published 2023
Paperback ISBN: 978-1-7394028-0-8
eBook ISBN: 978-1-7394028-1-5

Other

& DIFFERENT

An Anthology of Diverse Short Fiction

Edited by Dr Sarah Boyd

A Coup Of Owls Press

CONTENTS

Content Warnings

What Grief Tastes Like: Death, ableism.

Wreckwood: Vehicular wreck, asphyxiation.

Moons: Religious abuse, homophobia, suicidal thoughts.

The Kinsmen: Death, hauntings.

The Changeling of Sneem: Violence, blood.

Strawberry Hearts: Gore, Violence, Blood, Death, Psychological Abuse and Child Abuse.

Mitosis: Body horror, guts, purging, vomit, psychosis, implied violence.

Mermaid Tails and Tinfoil Hats: Suicide, death, mental illness, self-harm, discussions of abuse, institutionalisation.

Below The Horizon: Isolation, ableism.

The Shiny People: Social awkwardness and anxiety, earlier bereavement.

You See Food, You Eat It: Classism, sexual references.

Dear Name: Pregnancy.

Power To The People: Death, Misogyny, Islamophobia

FOREWORD

HERE we are in print! And we're hooting a joyful cacophony. (Yes, that's an oxymoron, but I don't care; we are all about 'other and different,' so our joy can get a little raucous!) We asked the forest for other and different, and you delivered. You ran at us full speed with your words, and we grabbed them, clasped them and consumed them.

Before writing this foreword, I looked up 'other' and 'different' in my tome of a dictionary. My favourite meaning of 'other' was: 'Different one or ones from that or those already specified or understood.' Meanwhile, my favourite for 'different' was: 'Out of the ordinary, unusual, other.' Like many of us, I've always felt other, out of and different from the ordinary. When I was younger, I had a stammer, a bad one, which meant communicating was a torturous experience; something as simple as saying my name became excruciating and embarrassing. Especially when I had to pause because my name had lodged itself in my oesophagus and refused to come out, and I got the response: 'Have you forgotten your name?'

I used to leap into books to escape into other worlds and away from this one where people didn't understand. But even in that escape, I still wanted to belong. I wanted to find my own gang of Others. If I found a character with a stammer that wasn't the butt of every joke, I rejoiced. But even better was finding another shy kid in the corner reading Point Horror (I'm showing my age now…) and asking if they'd read my favourite one and what their favourite was in return. I made the joyful discovery that, through the other and different (and through the wonder of fiction), we can find others who are different too. Isn't life, and language, clever?

We chose this theme for our first print issue because it encapsulates everything we stand for. We want to be here for all those outside the inside. In many parts of the world, being other or different can be life-threatening. We must champion the other and wave those multi-coloured flags as high and proud as possible. We must grasp onto being proud of ourselves and all the others who are like us and different from what is perceived as the 'norm.'

All of you lovely writers, readers and artists here with us in our owl-infested forest – I am proud of you. Look at these wonderful words you've crafted! Look at the stunning image on this glorious front cover! Look at this shiny book many of you gave your hard-earned money to support! It's beautiful, and you are beautiful. We appreciate every single one of you and want to wrap you in a warm, feathery hug in the centre of our deep, dark forest where you are always safe and loved.

My message to you is this: be different. Different from that or those already specified or understood. If you don't, who else will? We need you, all of you, to make the world a more interesting place. So, take a wing and come with us into the forest… be brave and proud… be other and be different… you'll fit right in.

RHIANNON WOOD - EIC

WRECKWOOD
Jonathan Olfert

By ancient law and common sense, you could only light a fire if you walked along the shore until you couldn't see home. Like most people, the Djeshi lived by the water, where a damp blanket or a leap into the surf might protect you. But a stray spark could still ignite the Watcher's Breath and burn a home right off its stilts or scour a family out of their cave.

Tole Sevenwrecks' luck was bad enough that he didn't just walk until all those nice families' homes were out of sight. He walked half the day across the top edge of the black rocks, in and out along the irregular coastline, before he dared to make a fire. And even then, he whispered useless charms with an eye on the Watcher, the dark shapelessness that squatted on the horizon, vast waves tickling at its haunches. It had the look of a statue, as if someone had carved a mountain into something like a man. The Breath wafted down the Watcher's slopes. Sometimes the Watcher moved.

By all forgotten gods... not tonight, I hope.

Ball clams would only crack under serious heat, and easier food was rare these days. Tole unwrapped his bundles – a dozen ball clams, a good weight of dry driftwood, and his carefully wrapped firestriker. The striker was a fork of springy whalebone that held a flint against a chunk of gleaming pyrite: as far as the Watcher's Breath ever let innovation get on these coasts. He'd gone far, to dangerous waters, looking for lands beyond the Breath and the Watcher's gaze. It hadn't ended well.

Tole arranged the clams on the driftwood and eased down the black rocks into the dangerous surf to wet his clothes and hair. Only once he was thoroughly non-flammable did he climb back up and smack the striker against a rock.

You could never tell if the Breath was drifting through the air. It didn't choke you or make you light-headed; it had no taste, no feel, no smell unless it was dense enough to become a shimmering fog. And that was the only time you'd see it. All along this coast, any spark, no matter how small, could set off an explosive burn.

Today was no exception. The striking surfaces cracked out a spark, then a WHUMPH that jolted Tole back on his heels. A burst of heat dried his eyes and baked his cheeks and forehead. Steam puffed out from his clothes to mingle with smoke and the stink of burnt arm hair. He stuffed his arm inside his wet coat: no harm done. The cookfire blazed angrily.

Chilly though he was, Tole sat a safe distance from the fire and watched the ball clams start to gape. Traces of the Watcher's Breath ignited at the edges of the cookfire, a little surge of brighter flame every few seconds.

Out past the smoke, over the sea, the Watcher brooded. The longer the cookfire burned, the heavier the clouds grew for leagues around the Watcher. These were low clouds, pregnant with Breath, fed by plumes of fog that rolled down from apertures in the Watcher's sloped head. If the storm grew taller, lightning would ignite it and burn it off in a firestorm, or rain might wash the Breath harmlessly into the sea.

The longer Tole sat there, the deeper his unease. The storm was staying low for now, growing dense and moving quickly toward shore. No rain, no lightning, just a huge knot of furious wind. That storm had all the markers of a bad night to come. The Watcher shifted, jarring distant waves. Perhaps the squatting inhuman god was anxious to share an uneasy sleep. The Watcher's Breath puffed out as great shimmering clouds, adding to the flammable storm.

Tole hurried back home as fast as he dared to move across the rocks and left the clams to burn.

~

The sky went dark early. By the time he reached town, Tole could barely see the path. Glowbee hives buzzed in an agitated way. Normally the hives ignored the Djeshi, but the dark, heavy air unsettled the glowbees. So did the hasty foot traffic along walkways that connected buildings and caves, and Tole heard more than one yelp from a sting. You could veil the hives and calm them with smoke, but the town needed the light. A storm demanded serious work: Djeshi workers were dampening everything soft, padding everything hard, filling clay jugs and great-shells with water, wrapping themselves in wet cloth, soaking thatched roofs, inflating breathing-skins in case fire ate the good air, and accounting for every single striker and piece of metal in town.

They'd all been through this a dozen times, but Tole knew fear when he saw it. By this point, the storm was visible from town as a wall of iridescent blue-grey, the densest Watcher's Breath in living memory. He'd moved fast; the storm had followed faster.

One spark and the whole Djeshi coast would burn.

~

He found his fellow loner Viir drinking in her boat, curled up on ragged fishing nets. The boat was her residence at the moment, tied up under the stilts of a wealthy whale hunter's home.

'Dark down here at the best of times,' Tole said, swinging down the stilts to land in the main hull. The bundled reeds bent under his weight, compressing against the wooden keel. 'Almost didn't see you.'

'And my boat would've been grateful,' said Viir. 'Jump around like that, you'll put a foot through the bottom. Thought you were grilling us dinner.'

'So did I. Clams didn't turn out, sorry.' Tole settled in beside the old fisherwoman and swiped her gourd away.

'Get your own, luckless,' she said without much fire. It stung anyway, the reminder that, yes, of every sailor on the Djeshi coast, Tole had the poorest share of fortune. Seven boats sunk since childhood, from tiny coracles to a raft with a deck fifteen trunks wide. His current lack of clams was all of a piece with that terrible luck. And she shouldn't have trusted him with their meal.

'My own wine?' Tole said. 'Not tonight. My own boat again? Ah, someday I'll get brave.' He gestured at the distant storm, what they could see of it under the houses at the edge of town. The waves were churning against the stilts. 'You seen what's coming, Auntie?'

Viir left the pile of nets to crouch in the bow and squint. 'Watcher's barnacled ass,' she spat, 'how long's that storm been there?'

Tole poured the wine over the edge and held the gourd underwater to fill. 'Let's get some water on your sails. Go on, jump in, or your clothes'll go up like tinder.'

'Storm that size takes a spark, we'll have bigger problems than the state of my clothes. A Breath burn only lasts a heartbeat, but the wind... the wind gets torn up just like the rest of us.' Viir slid over the edge and climbed right back in again, graceful despite age and intoxication.

Tole paused mid-pour. Water pooled on the folded sail and ran off into the bunched reeds of the deck. 'Viir...'

She tied back her bristly hair. 'What is it, boy?'

'We could spark it early.'

Viir barked a laugh. 'Where's the rest of my wine?' She scrabbled for her wineskin in the usual corners, then— 'Shit, you dumped it. You're not adding my boat to your seabed fleet, Tole. We'd burn, choke, drown if we're lucky.'

'I mean it, Viir.' Tole waved the gourd at the storm and the Watcher, shooing away an inquisitive glowbee. 'Just needs one spark, in there deep, before it reaches the coast. You can sail into the wind, I've seen you do it. You've got all the luck I never had.'

'Used to. I was a racer as a girl, ever tell you that?'

'That you used to be a girl?' he said. 'Once upon a time? I heard rumours.'

'Eh, shut your mouth.' Viir rubbed her eyes and stood to untie the boat's rope from the stilts. 'Sure, I'll do it, even if that's the wine talking. Wouldn't mind being the one to save the fancy folk who sneer at my fish and piss in my waves.'

Tole held up his wrapped whalebone-and-rock firestriker. 'You get me there, we bring a couple of breathing-skins, and I'll take care of the spark. Watcher's eyes, I won't lay a hand on your ropes, rudder, sails—'

Viir shoved the boat away from the stilts. '*You* may be cursed. Just this once, I'll make my luck enough for both of us.'

That hadn't worked out so well in the past. They'd fished and gathered and bartered together on occasion, and the best Tole could say of their collaboration was that they were both still alive. But something about this plan – did it count as naive if they knew it could kill? – brightened his mood better than anything in years.

~

Viir knew her boat. She held the ropes tight and tacked hard into the wind until the balsa-trunk outrigger rose higher than the sail. The slim reed craft skidded along the waves like its hull was fine-carved wood. Tole stayed low, clinging to the mast and whooping with joy.

He clung to that feeling as Viir tacked farther away from the coast, out where the spray ran cold. Schools of redfins rippled just under the surface, nervous, quick, with venom-tipped spines and gleaming scales. Deadly waters, even for an experienced sailor with Viir's luck. Tole squinted through the spray, looking for the tiny islands that studded the sea between the coast and the Watcher's base. But the waves were starting to crest, and the rocks blended in with the grey water.

Ideas rushed through his head as he curled up around the base of the mast. With the right stones, whalebone or drums, you could set up a... he didn't have a word for it. A thing that would spark when the wind rose high. These rocky little islands had crevices, didn't they? Places to funnel the wind but keep such an invention from washing away, shield it from the Watcher's gaze?

Ideas for another time, if time allowed. Tonight it didn't.

The Watcher, veiled by gloom, shifted behind the clouds. Torrential wind caught the inflated breathing-skins and tore them free of their wrappings and ties. Viir howled something. Tole swiped seawater from his eyes and crawled back toward the rudder to hear.

The implication of losing the skins was settling in, and the storm loomed high. He hoped Viir had hope to offer.

'Cut the outrigger loose, luckless!' Viir yelled over the wind. 'Wreck another boat! Do it!'

She braced the rudder with her knee and handed Tole a knife. It was a good one: clean lines, strong flint core, anchored to a driftwood handle with seaweed cord and pine pitch... and keen enough to bleed him out if he looked at it wrong.

He gripped it so tight he half forgot to grip the boat. The reed hull grated across merciless water at a speed he'd rarely matched in a good boat with the wind at his back. But Viir slowed down, steering toward the bulk of the storm, and the outrigger dipped until the waves caught it. The ragged reed boat lined up with the Watcher at the storm's heart.

Wind caught the sail and wrenched the rope along Viir's forearm, but she held on. The boat leaped forward at a steep slant that the outrigger would have prevented.

Watcher's Breath had a faint scent when it got dense enough, like green coconut water gone sour. 'I smell it!' Tole shouted back at Viir. Elbow looped around the mast, he fished for the wrapped striker in his coat. He came up empty. The inflated skins weren't the only tools they'd lost.

He caught a glimpse of Viir's eyes gone wide, mouth open round in a yell, and then the boat came apart under them.

Broken reeds stabbed and scraped through his clothes. The wooden keel spun free like a bird hunter's throwing stick. The waves smashed Tole's skull two, three times before he slowed enough to sink. Something rough rasped the skin off his arm – rope or reeds or bristly hair, moving fast.

Seawater jammed itself up his nostrils like hooked fingers and jerked his head down. Tole found himself trapped in a cycle of snorting and choking as he fought for the surface with no clear sense of where it was.

His elbow cracked against the mast. He retained enough sense to grab it and throw a leg over. Cold wind bit through his wet clothes from head to toe, but at least he'd found air.

He inhaled a gallon of spray before he got his first clear breath. The current yanked him one way, the wind another, and the mast moved independently. Held firm, rather, and he realized the mast had embedded itself between sharp, implacable rocks.

~

Apart from a jagged spine of boulders, the tiny island lurked below the surface on a calm day. Tonight, the storm dragged waves up and shoved the water down deep, exposing rock dotted with the splinters of ancient wrecks. The carcass of the boat wrapped itself around the crags among its predecessors. Viir hung from a tangle of sails, spinning in the wind, suspended from the bloody rope around her left arm. The way she dangled said she'd dislocated the arm, maybe worse.

As Tole clambered from the mast into the boulders, though, Viir snagged a tangle of seaweed to halt her spin and pulled herself up until the rope relaxed enough to slip free. Tole skinned both knees rushing to catch Viir before she collapsed.

They skidded into a prickly, slippery tidepool among high boulders that offered reasonable shelter from the waves. They caught their breath, let their hearts slow down as torn sails whipped overhead. The smell of Breath hung thick in the air.

'One spark,' Viir said, pain heavy in her voice. 'Lost your striker?'

Tole shook his head. 'No. I mean, yes, I lost it, but we need a plan to survive.'

Viir choked a laugh. 'Do we? What plan could there be, hm?' She jostled him. 'Eh, luckless? You believe we're...'

The wind stole the rest of what she said. Tole gripped the old fisherwoman's good hand in hopes of giving and receiving reassurance.

'We can still survive this,' he said, and tried very hard to believe it.

'No.' Viir closed her eyes. 'You need to understand we'll probably die very, very soon. Not a bad way to go, but go we will.' She let go of Tole's hand to scrabble for stones in the tidepool. A simple rock-against-rock spark would ignite the Breath storm easily enough.

'Wait, wait,' Tole said, grabbing her arm. 'We can trap good air between our coats and the water, like a tent.'

Viir shook off his hand but didn't bash her chosen rock against the tidepool's edge. Not yet. 'You came out here to make heroes of us,' she said irritably. 'What'd you think that looks like? You think they'll sing songs about the old trash-fish catcher who hid under a coat?'

Wind and tears prickled in Tole's eyes. 'Didn't think you were coming out here to die.'

'Tole, our coats were ragged enough before the wreck. They won't hold air; they might not even keep the fire out. And that's assuming the fire burns quick. But two wet coats layered might protect one of us. You should get under there; I'll set the spark. Give me this. Let me have this.'

That sounded like the wine talking, but she hadn't drunk that much, had she? No, this was old pain, a desperate sacrifice for scraps of respect, and Tole Sevenwrecks couldn't fault her a bit.

'The sail whipping around up there,' Tole said. 'There's a rope off the end.' He got up and shrugged out of his coat. Sore as he was, he could still move, still climb. 'Sure, we'll probably die, but...'

'But what?'

He shook his head and started climbing the boulders despite the ache in his knees, ignoring the impassive gaze of the shape behind the clouds. 'You've been drinking to the wrong songs, Viir.'

~

Seven wrecks, some of them brutal and flat-out hopeless, had left him with more than just a reputation. As he climbed, he got a sense of the sail's position, what anchored it, how intact it was, and how to approach it. There wasn't much left of his fingertips by the time he caught the sail's edge. He lost a fingernail pulling it down against the wind and another snaring the rope. With a glance down at Viir in the tidepool, Tole wrapped the rope around his arm from elbow to wrist.

The sail, still caught in the highest rocks, was more than long enough to let him reach the tidepool again. He climbed down, bringing the end of the sail

with him. The boulders hid him from the Watcher –
that felt like it mattered – but offered minimal shelter
from the wind. The storm threatened to whip him out
from the island, clear off the ground.

Viir struggled to her feet and gripped the rope
with her good arm. They hauled together, trying to
drag it down far enough to tent it over the tidepool,
but the top end of the sail held firm.

They yelled back and forth in the height of the
storm, spreading out the sail against the tidepool. In
the end, the best they could manage was a vertical
cocoon of sorts, twisted against the side of the
boulders.

Once they'd wrapped themselves together in the
sail, Tole squeezed his arm out with a hard rock in
his fist. He braced his wrist against the boulder.
'Ready?' he said against the top of his old friend's
head.

Viir's breath – wine and bad teeth – filled the
sailcloth cocoon. 'Make us a spark,' she said. 'No,
wait, wait.'

Tole froze. 'What?'

'I can still smell it,' Viir said. 'The air in here's
half Breath.'

'Wet sail should douse it.'

'Sure,' she said, 'but not before it burns the good
out of the air.' She struggled out of the cocoon and
pawed her eyes. 'Agh, that's Watcher's own mercy,
that is. I don't want you to burn, kid.'

'So...' Tole stayed in the twisted sail, mostly to
keep it from blowing away like all his ideas.

'Get under the coats,' Viir said, 'down in the pool. Go on, hurry. Wait too long, and the fire'll catch the village anyway.'

Tole squinted toward the coast, or the direction he thought was the coast. The iridescent storm had killed visibility and left the ocean darker than midnight. At least midnight had stars.

'You're right,' Tole said. 'We're out of time. Hold our breath and get in the water?'

Viir laughed and spat blood and laughed again. 'Won't that be a terrible song.'

They crawled into the tidepool and pulled the wet coats over themselves. Tole tented them with his elbow, filling a little space with air that stank of Breath. The firestorm would probably ignite it, but maybe not. Maybe.

Under the water, he and Viir clasped each other's hands briefly. Then he reached out and hammered a stone against the rocks of the tidepool until they gave birth to a tiny little spark.

~

Ignition crushed the coats flat, slammed him down against the jagged floor of the tidepool, and heated the water from cold to scalding. Light speared through gaps in the coats. Like any Djeshi, he could hold his breath longer than most, but the firestorm went on and on.

Air squeezed out between his teeth and lips. He tried to trick his mind by breathing out into his mouth and in again, panting, giving his lungs a full range of motion. When that stopped working, he began to exhale a bit at a time. No relief lasted long. He dreamed wildly of opening his lips, of fire burning deep in his lungs.

Viir gripped Tole's shoulder until her fingernails bit through the skin, maybe in a struggle for control, maybe just to keep him from surging up through the wet coats. But as the surface clouded with wriggling steam, her grip slackened, then tightened, then slackened again. Then it was Tole's turn to hold her down until she could get control again.

The light died out, and the heat slackened. The air was always bad after a large Breath burn. Right now, Tole craved even bad air. The good would come soon enough, rushing in to replace the bad. Wouldn't it?

Viir's grip relaxed, became a shove, and Tole clawed his way free of the coats. Hot wind baked his face and set his clothes steaming. He dragged Viir up to her feet. Then and only then did he let himself take a breath. His chest unclamped like a clam in a cookfire.

He opened his eyes as smoky air filled his lungs, the remains of the boat. Steam rose from the ocean all around, far ahead and far back out to sea. Wisps played around the base, the haunches, of the vast shape there.

The burn had scoured the Watcher's Breath from the air and left the sky... not bright, not black, just a gently clouded evening. The Watcher settled as if resting or watching closer. Smoke spiralled up from the near edges of the coast. Farther away, angry glowbees swirled in the Djeshi harbour, but no smoke. Not even steam. The ash of reeds and sailcloth fluttered in the air.

The distant Djeshi unfurled from their hiding places to find themselves alive. Some, perhaps, were staring out across the water at a small and smoking island and the two fools standing on its rocks.

Truth be told, Tole didn't like his odds of getting gratitude or of tomorrow being different than yesterday. But he'd know, wouldn't he, that all those proud folk owed him their lives. He'd know it forever.

'That,' rasped Viir, 'looks like a long cold swim.' She laughed under her breath and straightened up, bright-eyed and eager, more alive now than he'd ever seen. 'Eh, maybe not that cold.'

JONATHAN OLFERT

Jonathan Olfert (he/they) is a neurodivergent Canadian writer who dabbles in fantasy, sci-fi, weird horror, and paleofiction. Their stories have backstabbed and skulked their way into reputable establishments like *Beneath Ceaseless Skies*, *Interzone*, and *Old Moon Quarterly*. He and his partner live in unceded Mi'kmaq territory near Halifax.

WHAT GRIEF TASTES LIKE
Avra Margariti

THE girl looks around eleven. She's skittish, gazing around the cottage with fearful curiosity. Lenore can't really blame her. After all, she moved her potion-making business near the girl's town only three months ago. People are always hesitant to trust a witch, especially one as young as Lenore, even when they are in need of said witch's services. Lenore studies the slip of paper with the neat, lace-like penmanship she assumes belongs to the girl's mother. The contents of the note make her heart stumble, just a little, as its hollow beats echo in her ears.

A gasp flies past the girl's lips. Looking up, Lenore sees what has captured her attention. It's not the long strings of dried herbs tied together with red and white twine, the collection of mortars and pestles, or the shelves of glass vials filled with potions of all colours perceived by the human eye.

'Don't worry, he's harmless.' Lenore nods toward the large snake wrapped four or five times around a table leg as he naps in the slanted sunlight. 'His name is Adam.'

The girl sucks in her bottom lip. 'He? Is he your familiar, then?'

Lenore averts her eyes from the girl's wide-eyed stare. 'Something like that.'

'Can I pet him?'

The coils of Adam's body undulate; he withdraws into the muted, grainy shadows with a soft susurration of displeasure.

'Better not, love.' Lenore tucks the piece of paper under a pile of grimoires and old botanical tomes. 'Go home to your mother now but come back here at the end of the week. The potion will be ready then.'

The girl darts one last look under the table. Then she steps through the cottage's arched doorway, heading down the overgrown forest path that will eventually lead her back into town.

Lenore leans against her workbench and rubs her fists against her eyes. They're tired suddenly. As dry as book dust. The potion is going to be a difficult one. She can't make it on her own, not without hurting herself.

'Adam,' Lenore says. 'Please. I need you.'

At first, she thinks he won't listen. Each time, it takes him longer to come back to her. The snake's body slithers with only a whisper of sound across the bare wooden floorboards. His black scales reflect the afternoon sunlight, casting minuscule, fractured rainbows around the room. The sight makes Lenore's breath catch in her throat.

She blinks, and a young man sits curled on the floor where the snake just was, his mahogany hair messy and his lanky limbs tangled together.

'What is it?' Adam asks sullenly.

His pupils are no longer slitted and vertical; his golden irises morph back into warm brown as he blinks, becoming accustomed to his body again. His human form retains some of the reptilian mannerisms, though. When he pulls out a chair and sits down, every one of his movements is fluid: a meandering stream.

'Adam, I need your help with a potion. I can't prepare it alone.'

Lenore bites the pink inside of her cheek. Again, she fears Adam will refuse.

'Of course,' he says, softening. 'Anything you want.'

She writes a list of ingredients using yellow parchment and a quill, all the while making sure to keep Adam in her line of vision. She's trying to prolong the moment, keep human-form Adam tethered to her side a little while longer.

'Lenore?' he says when he's almost at the door. Already his skin is rippling. His nose flattens, his tongue splitting down the middle to form its serpentine fork.

'Yes?'

'You called me your familiar earlier.'

There's no judgement in his hissing-soft voice, but Lenore still burns with shame. 'I didn't mean it that way. It was just something to say.'

'Well, I'm not. Not less than what I wasss. Not less than anyone elssse. Remember thisss for me.' Adam is known to drag and whistle his sibilants when he's upset, and now is no exception.

'I know,' she says, pushing back the prickly tears that threaten to spill over. 'I'm sorry.'

And she does know. Adam is her best friend, her equal. So what if he chooses to spend most of his days in his snake form, crawling along the rafters or basking in the sun? He always slips into the forest at dawn so that when Lenore wakes up, dog's breath, eye of newt, and other roots and flowers still wet with dew await her on her potion-making station. He's here for her when she needs him.

Lenore can respect Adam's own needs, even though she doesn't always understand them. Yet, she slipped up again. She keeps breaking the heart she vowed to protect.

~

In the dark, narrow pupils swim in cauldrons of molten gold, reminiscent of Lenore's early alchemy days. She rolls over, allowing Adam to slither up her bed and align his body with hers. This is something they've been doing long before they moved into the cottage in the forest together. Now, they have all the more reason for it. Adam doesn't have control over his temperature in this form, so Lenore lets him snuggle close and soak up her warmth.

The first part of the potion for the little girl's mother is complete. The dark liquid ferments on the windowsill. It smells faintly of liquorice and sulphur. Lenore and Adam, after pouring so much of their powers into its preparation, are left hollowed out and aching all over.

'Adam, talk to me,' she pleads.

His forked tongue flickers out of his mouth. He must taste Lenore's anxiety permeating the air because he goes from serpent to human again, from freezing cold to furnace hot.

'I'm tired,' he says.

Lenore is, too. Every one of her muscles feels pulverized and tender, and she hasn't been able to leave the bed all day. The last time she felt so exhausted to her core, she had helped prepare a different potion, one that would allow Adam to turn into a snake at will. 'If you don't help me, I'm going to disappear into the woods, and you'll never see me again,' he had threatened. And Lenore cried because he wasn't being fair. Yet, she'd still helped him attain what he said he needed most.

Adam used to say things like, *The lights are too loud,* or, *All these people are making it hard to breathe*. His senses were an exposed nerve, the universe streaming into him, howling and unfiltered.

Lenore asks into the inky darkness, 'Do you remember when we used to hide in the forest and practice our spells and potions?'

He settles closer to her. 'Yes. We made everyone mad with worry trying to find us.'

She strokes Adam's arm in the firm, deep touches she knows he enjoys on warm skin and sleek scales alike. 'What about the pillow forts we used to make when we were children?'

Adam's laughter vibrates against her. 'Of course I remember, Lenore. *Everything.* You were trying to keep the world out. You did it for me, and it helped.'

'I don't know if I did the right thing. Then, and now, too.'

Lenore thinks of the transfiguration potion again. Should she have helped Adam retreat into himself for his own comfort, or should she seek to change the world, one spell, one potion at a time, so it better accommodates him?

'You were only doing what I asked of you, like friends do.' He bumps their foreheads together.

'Now, stop thinking and go to sleep. Our work isn't done – you'll need your strength tomorrow.'

~

Adam and Lenore stand before their cottage's widest window, watching the girl go. The opaque bottle containing the brewed medicine is clasped tight between her hands. Her steps are long and springy as if she's barely holding back from breaking into a sprint. Adam insisted that they shouldn't accept payment for this particular concoction, and Lenore couldn't deny him his request.

'Do you think her mother stands a chance now?' Adam asks, his voice as careful as if they were back at their workstation, measuring ingredients with no room for mistakes.

Dappled sunlight filters in through the gaps in the crocheted curtains, flitting across their skin. Still, Lenore shivers. 'She's going to be okay. They caught the illness early, and the potion will help her body fight it off. It's not like last time.'

'Like my mother, you mean.' Adam's tongue wisps out into the air as if he's forgotten the form he's in.

Lenore wonders what grief tastes like. It must be salty like the tears currently gathering in the corners of her eyes. Or perhaps it carries a sour bite, like the smell of a sick body too weary to keep fighting. Adam's mother's illness had progressed to its final stage when a doctor finally diagnosed her. Over and over again, Lenore and Adam had offered to make a potion for her, but she was adamant in her refusal.

She didn't want to hurt them, she said. And so, Adam's mother had braced herself and faced the end with not a drop of magic in her body.

'I miss her too,' Lenore says, leaning against the windowsill beside Adam.

His voice is so soft she almost thinks the wind is replying for him. 'I know.'

'And I know she was the only person who could make you want to try. To stay in your current form, to not escape the loudness.' The tears are free-falling now, and Lenore doesn't try to stop them. 'Just as I know I'm not enough to fill the void she left behind.'

'Not true,' Adam spits in his hurry to get the words out. 'Any of it.'

'I don't mind if it is. We all cope in different ways.'

'I don't want to ssstay in my sssnake form forever,' he bites out, face twisted in frustration. 'But it feelsss… sssafe. Peaceful, even. For now.'

Lenore remembers the last thing Adam's mother told them. 'Take care of each other's hearts, my loves. Don't let the world crack them open.'

Lenore's heart feels vitreous. She's beginning to understand why Adam has been so quick to change into his snake form lately. Why he would want to ball up every emotion, every stimulus, until they're small and tight and bearable.

'Anything you need,' Lenore says. 'Whenever you're ready. I love you.'

'And I, you,' he replies. They don't feel the need to name the kind of love inhabiting the grief-hollow places inside them these past few months. After all, it's always lived there between them, sun-warm and many-formed.

Adam squeezes her hand once, hard, before shedding his skin. He goes from boy to serpent, opaline-bellied and smooth-scaled, elegantly slithering into the dark green of the forest.

Once she is alone, Lenore wanders over to her various shelves. The wood bends and groans under the weight of glass and paper. In the very back, she finds the potion she brewed for Adam three months ago, right after his mother had returned to the earth's moss-soft cradle. She rolls the small vial between her palms. Adam once told her the cottage tastes of tea, herbs and sunlit dust on his forked tongue. He said that in his snake form, his thoughts are a comforting balm, not more or less than what they were before but easier to examine and compartmentalize: *eat, slither, play, bask, breathe breathe keep breathing through the pain.*

Think of LenoreLenoreLenore.

Smiling softly, Lenore uncaps the vial and lifts it to her nostrils. She pictures herself slithering out into the forest after Adam. The two of them twisting around each other in sweet-smelling fields of aster flowers. Later, when they're ready, brewing tea, stories and potions in their cosy cottage together. Girl and snake, or girl and boy, or two snakes, sleek and rainbowed. *Whatever you need.*

She doesn't swallow the contents of the vial, not before she talks with Adam about it. But Lenore can already feel the sun on her scales, the forest filling their hearts with quiet.

AVRA MARGARITI

Avra Margariti is a queer author, Greek sea monster, and Pushcart-nominated poet with a fondness for the dark and the darling. Avra's work haunts publications such as *Vastarien, Asimov's, Liminality, Arsenika, The Future Fire, Space and Time, Eye to the Telescope,* and *Glittership*. "The Saint of Witches", Avra's debut collection of horror poetry, is available from Weasel Press.

You can find Avra on twitter (@avramargariti).

MOONS
Miriam H. Harrison

THEY told her of the world, of how it existed in a union of complements. Day and night. Sun and moon. Man and woman. These things balanced each other, depended on each other, defined each other by their difference.

'The way of the universe,' they said. 'The way it was intended.'

But she didn't see their universe. She lived beneath a sky that did not dim or brighten between the pulls of day and night. Her sky was ever-painted in streaks of orange, white, and pink.

Looking up, she saw the light of two moons, both full and complete.

~

When she was little, she loved gazing up into the warm colours of her sky, the steady glow of her moons. It was a beautiful sight, bright with possibility. Anything was possible under her sky.

It took time to learn that something was wrong. She asked her mother once how far away the moons were.

'Moons?' Her mother's brow furrowed. She seemed tense, angry. 'Surely you mean *the* moon?'

She nodded, and her mother softened. Her mother gave an answer, but she didn't hear it. She thought instead of her mother's furrowed brow, wondered what was wrong with her moons.

~

She did not speak of her sky. Instead, she nodded to their stories of sunrises and sunsets, of the blue and sunshine of their so-called daylight. She pretended these things were there in the sky above her, pretended they had meaning, pretended they told of her place in the world.

The others liked her quiet listening, liked that she did not ask too many questions or presume to have any answers. This was part of her place, part of where she fit in their stories of day and night, sun and moon.

Alone, she looked to her moons and wondered.

~

She learned there were words for her sky, but none dared speak them. Her moons were a violation, a desecration of the balance of complements. They had no place in the blue-sky universe.

Only the blue sky shone with golden holiness. All around her, others lifted their hands high, gloried in its light. She followed their lead, reaching high, grasping at the chance to share in the promise of an unseen sun.

She looked up with a wild hunger, hoping the sky might yet open bright and blue above her. But always, her moons confirmed her silent shame.

~

Living under the wrong sky, she felt alone in the crowds of familiar faces. She went through the motions of connecting, believing, belonging while knowing there was no place for her among them. Though their smiling faces seemed so near, she knew they were worlds apart. She knew their smiles would not last if she spoke honestly of her pink-hued sky, her double moons. They did not know her – they knew only her carefully tended silence.

Still, she went through the motions, hoping she might one day truly belong. Hoping she might find their sky or that they would stop hating hers.

~

Sometimes she saw the gleam of her moons in others. Sometimes she would see another girl with the light of two moons beckoning in her eyes. Sometimes their gazes would meet, would linger, would consider each other. Sometimes the girl might smile, her moonbeam eyes shining with recognition and possibility.

In those moments, she felt a fluttering in her stomach: the thrill and terror of falling. But each time, she turned away, resisting the pull of eyes that had seen the sky of two moons.

Alone, she fell to her knees, begging the forgiveness of a sky she'd never seen.

~

She stumbled under the weight of her moons. They were a heavy secret to bear, and she tired of carrying it. She knew there was safety in silence, yet sometimes a question would break through her defences.

'What if someone can't help it?' she asked once. 'What if they just can't see the sun?'

'Ignoring the sun is a choice,' the blue-sky believer replied. 'There is only one sky.'

'How can you be sure?' she asked, with immediate regret. Again, she saw the furrowed brow, the sharpened eye of their hostility.

'There is only one sky,' they repeated.

~

And so, she spent more time inside, away from her double moons. The world inside was dim and lonely, but at least she could ignore those things she could not change, pretend she was as she should be. When she did venture out, she would not look up from the ground, could not bear to look up into her shame. Try as she might, she could not pray away the sky – always, it was there, out of reach of her self-loathing, their judgment.

They had made it clear that only one world was worth living in – and it wasn't hers.

~

Was it worth the trouble? The silence that weighed on her, the loneliness that saddened her, the shame that haunted her, the fear that hunted her. Was living really worth the trouble?

Knowing of the blue sky, knowing she had never seen it, knowing she could only ever pretend – was this even life? If she did not live in their world, if their world was the only one that mattered, what did her life matter? Could she only ever pretend to matter?

They had given her answers, answers that confirmed her worthlessness. What she needed was a question worth asking.

~

'Do you really believe?'

He asked as though it were a simple thing, but the question shook her.

'What do you mean?'

He gestured to the crowds, their arms reaching for an unseen sun. 'They speak with so much certainty. Do you believe?'

She considered. His was a new face here among the believers. Among them, but not one of them. None of the others had asked if she believed – they had only told her that she must. She had never seen him before, would never see him again, but here he was with a question.

Do you really believe?

~

The question did not give her answers. It did not presume to know. Instead, it glowed with a strange illumination – a light that did not show her the way but revealed the curves of her inner labyrinth.

She realized for the first time how many twists and turns entrapped her, how far removed she was from happiness by a maze of misplaced certainties. There was no quick way back.

But above it all was her sky, her moons. They glowed as they always had, both full and complete. And she knew again that anything was possible under her sky.

MIRIAM H. HARRISON

Miriam H. Harrison writes strange and wondrous things from her home hidden among the boreal forests and abandoned mines of Northern Ontario. She is a regular contributor to *Pen of the Damned*, and updates about her published works can be found at miriamhharrison.wordpress.com

THE KINSMEN
Busayo Akinmoju

THE king dies.

And then, that day, a small storm of bats tears through the greying skies. The children stop in the middle of their play, laughing at it. Pointing at the drunken, graceless wings as they swim above. They think it is just birds. The children think they are birds, brief visitors on their annual migratory path.

But someone's mother comes out of the house, drying her hands on a cloth. She sees what they are pointing at and exclaims at their irreverence.

'Can't you see it's bats? Stop that right now.'

The children are confused, but the stern look on the woman's face is enough to stop their laughing.

They don't understand; they think it is just birds on their annual migratory path.

The children see the fear creep over the mother's face. The woman's eyes fill with the image of bat wings floating in the sky like a stream of ash.

These aren't birds, but they are migrating. From one empty cave to another. From one life under the cave of death.

Something has shifted in all their lives now, and the woman looks at the empty, still-smiling faces of the children. They do not understand.

~

The first thing that happens when a king dies is not the burial.

The people do not mourn him or weep for him. There is nothing to mourn; he is a person re-joining the line of his ancestors. The more important thing is to prevent the world from tearing apart once he dies. And that only happens if he cannot make that journey back home into the afterlife.

If he doesn't go back, the small tear in the fabric between the two worlds caused by his death grows. And then, one wandering spirit walks into this world, one after the other. Killing people, destroying the market structure, painting the world with plagues.

No one wants that to happen, so once the king dies, the first thing the Kingmakers do is to make preparations for his journey.

Segi, the Chief Kingmaker, is weaving a basket when the king dies. Even when she feels the uncomfortable shift of the world's fabric ripping, she isn't surprised by it.

Being Chief Kingmaker is a role that comes with the power of divination. She knew when the king would die the moment the role was handed to her seven years ago. She had seen it clearly – the king would go on an ill-advised trip to see a woman who wasn't his and get bitten by a snake as he made his way through the forest back home. And he would die within a week.

Still, she'd had to wait. Segi had to hold that dread that she would have to fulfil her role as Chief Kingmaker many years younger than anyone else before her. The dread was from knowing she had to make the ultimate sacrifice once she carried out her role.

When the Kingmakers install a new king, the Chief Kingmaker drops her mortal body too. Dies and joins the line of other chiefs, not her ancestors – which would be more pleasant, Segi thinks. Instead, she joins all the other Chief Kingmakers that came before her.

A very cold and unfeeling set of people, Segi thinks to herself as she remembers her years of training.

Segi completes the basket she is weaving.

'Right in time,' she says to herself. And throws ash into the small fire burning in front of her. And with that, she releases the bats into the sky.

~

Segi can't start the meeting until everyone is present.

Only the Iyaloja is missing.

She looks around herself; all of the other Kingmakers are seated, all seven of them. With their hair threaded into small puffs and coral beads woven in tiny intricacies across their scalps. They look beautiful with the hairstyle of the sorority, Segi muses.

She had taken out that same hairstyle earlier that evening, and her hair is loosened now, tucked away under a tight scarf. Not a single hair in sight. Soon, when she stands before the king's spirit during the ritual, her head will be shaved bald. She has to become like a spirit in order to stand before a spirit.

Become elemental and forsake all human concerns like hairstyles, expensive coral beads, or emotion.

Segi decides not to think about that.

Instead, like all of the other Kingmakers, she begins to wonder where the Iyaloja is, the last person needed to make their circle nine and begin the preparation for the summoning of the king's spirit.

'Abi, she is not coming again?' one of the Kingmakers asks.

The others hum in agreement with the question, everyone wondering what is taking the Iyaloja so long.

Segi cannot answer the question, but she begins to consider that the unsettled feeling in her chest is about more than just the king's passing. Or the dread she feels about the impending journey they will both take.

When Segi set the bats free on the day the king died, it hadn't happened the way the Chief Kingmaker who trained her explained it would. What Segi expected was for a single bat to come out of the flame when she threw the ash in, and once it flew out into the sky, it would rip into the tiny storm of fluttering wings that the town would see, letting them know what had happened.

Several bats had come out of the flame instead, the same size as the bits of ash Segi had thrown in, and they had swelled in size as they tore violently out of the room.

She runs the thought over in her mind, but she tells herself it could have been anything; maybe she had forgotten what the former Chief Kingmaker had said. Segi remembers her reluctance to learn her lessons then, how much she had missed her family. She could have mixed things up. She could have.

They continue waiting, but the Iyaloja doesn't come. They wait several hours before Segi decides to tell everyone to go home. The other Kingmakers leave, not without some quiet comments about rudeness and people learning to respect others' time.

Segi's unsettled feeling grows. She knows that the Iyaloja understands the importance of time when it comes to this situation. If the Iyaloja didn't come, she likely had a reason.

Although reluctant, that reason is something Segi has to know.

~

'Segilola,' the Iyaloja says.

And Segi knows things have taken an interesting turn. No one has called her by her given name in years.

'Segilola,' the Iyaloja repeats.

She has no choice but to answer. Even though the Iyaloja is older than her, Segilola outranks all the other chiefs in the king's court. The person who dies with the king and ensures his journey home can only be an equal to the king. Everyone accepts this, even if very few say it.

So Segi wonders why the Iyaloja doesn't use the more deferential *menne* to address her.

Menne, my mother. Or to the rest of the kingdom, *menwe,* our mother.

'I'm listening,' Segi finally answers.

'Good,' the Iyaloja says, then she turns to the other people in the room and motions for them to leave.

When they are finally alone, the Iyaloja sizes Segi up and down through narrowed eyes and says, 'Segilola, I have known you since you were little. In fact, since you were born. The moment I set eyes on you, no one had to tell me what your destiny would look like. Even before the diviners had spelled out your destiny to us, I knew you were our Chief Kingmaker.'

She pauses to watch Segi's face for a moment.

'But,' the Iyaloja says, 'no one could have told us you would come into the role at such a crucial and precarious time in our kingdom.'

'What do you mean?' Segi asks.

The Iyaloja releases a sigh and looks away from Segi, turning her head to stare through the window at the now perfect-blue sky outside.

'How do I tell you this, my daughter?' she says with a tenderness that Segi is unused to from her.

She finally continues, 'You know I did not come for the meeting with you and the Kingmakers. And I know that, ultimately, is why you are here.'

Segi nods.

'Well, I did not come because of another meeting. While the king was ill, I and the other palace chiefs decided – based on what the people had been requesting - that if the king passed on to his ancestors, we would need to decide if we – if the kingdom – really need a new king after all.'

'What?' Segi exclaims, standing up.

The Iyaloja's words are a loud thud in her ears. How could they decide such a thing? If there was no new king, then there was no way for the current king to pass on. If he didn't, the fabric of the world, torn open now, would grow into something irreparable.

They are playing with forces more powerful than any human. Segi stops pacing around the room and stares at the older woman, expecting an explanation.

Nothing.

~

The king appears to Segi the night after she leaves the Iyaloja's house.

He does not appear as a spirit, which Segi expected to happen if she ever saw him outside of his lifetime.

He comes into the fire in the middle of her hut.

She wakes up suddenly, stirred not by a sound but by a palpable presence watching her. Her eyes adjust to the darkness, searching out light, and she sees him in the fire. An amorphous shape flickering within the flame. But Segi knows it is him; she sees the long crease that runs between his eyebrows. She sees the deep set to his eyes – unmistakable in their intent.

And Segi, looking into those eyes, realises that she stands not before a dead king but an exiled one.

A man exiled from his kingdom.

She thinks about what the Iyaloja said about the kingdom not wanting a king anymore. In deciding this, Segi realised that the people had not only set up the world for danger, but they had sent their king into limbo. Wandering in the uncomfortable space between this life and the next.

They had made him half-human and half-spirit at the same time. Making a king hang around in shadows and flames, hoping his people would do the right thing for him.

In realising this, Segi sees the limited power of the office of a king. Despite his wealth, his influence and his role in the kingdom, what is a king without a kingdom to rule? Without a people agreeing to be ruled by him.

And Segi thinks about herself – what is a Kingmaker, Chief Kingmaker or otherwise, without a king to serve? Her duty has been her whole life, and now, nothing stands before her. What is her purpose without this role she had prepared her whole life for?

Looking into the flames, she sees that the king has exiled her as much as he has exiled himself.

They are outsiders to their own kingdom now, effectively without a people and therefore without a reason for being.

All because he couldn't control himself, Segi thinks bitterly. She looks into the flicker of the fire and feels, for the first time, the same rage and disappointment that the whole kingdom had felt when they realised what the king had done. Why he died.

Was he worth serving? Segi asks.

Someone who could open them up to attack from neighbouring kingdoms, someone who could leave the government without direction, only to go after what wasn't his?

Were kings worth it? Giving all that power to only one person.

Segi stops looking into the flame because she does not like the answer she comes up with. She pivots away from the fire, ignoring the nagging presence it holds and goes back to bed, turning her back firmly against the flame.

~

A month later, the king still hasn't joined his ancestors.

But the people finally converge to decide kingly matters.

Half of the kingdom stands in the forest of the ancestors, where people are buried, where kings are sent off home. They all listen as the Iyaloja addresses them.

Segi used to think it would be a dark, eerie place. That the air would be humid, heavy with the presence of the dead hanging between the trees. But it is an almost arid landscape. Red earth, hot sun and thin, wispy trees swaying in the dry, intermittent breeze.

She sits on a grey stone, the only one allowed to sit in the presence of the ancestors. And waits for the Iyaloja to call her up.

Over the past weeks, Segi has often woken up in the middle of the night. Not because of the king appearing in a flame but a cold fear that would not let her sleep.

With the people deciding to no longer be ruled by a king, her role in the kingdom is no longer defined. And even worse, she stands a risk of being attacked.

Many of the other Kingmakers have reported the whisperings they have heard around the kingdom. There are plots to harm anyone considered sympathetic to the continuity of rule under a king.

Many of the palace chiefs are targets. Members of the royal family have gone into hiding, so a new king cannot even be chosen. And Segi, being the closest to the king in both spirit and death, is not safe. Neither are the other Kingmakers.

They often have to meet in secret now. When an invitation for a meeting was extended to them from the Iyaloja, Segi half-expected it to be an ambush. That she and the seven other Kingmakers would be lined up and killed. But the Iyaloja came to Segi's hut, alone and bearing no arms, and spoke to Segi softly like the old friends they were. Segi decided to listen to whatever her offer was and invited the other Kingmakers.

When the Kingmakers arrived at Segi's hut, they did not come without hostility towards the Iyaloja, who they all considered to be a traitor in their ranks.

The Iyaloja knew this and considered it in her approach to them when the Kingmakers arrived.

'My Kingmakers,' she had said. 'Today, I come to you in person, I greet you.' And the Iyaloja knelt before them.

The Kingmakers gasped, seeing an older woman kneel before them, an abomination. A few of them rushed to get her to stand up.

Once the Iyaloja was on her feet again and saw the sympathetic edge to the Kingmakers' countenances, she began to lay out her offer.

'My Kingmakers, many of you might be aware of how the kingdom sees you now. As plotters, as people insistent on the old ways under a king who brought nothing but harm to us. But I, your Iyaloja, do not see that.'

The Iyaloja proceeded, saying, 'I consider myself one of you. After all, I am just as much a Kingmaker as you are. A king cannot be chosen without someone who will run his market structures, who will coordinate the wealth that comes into the kingdom through trade. That is the role of the Iyaloja, and that is what I do and why I am Kingmaker too.'

The Kingmakers nodded, and Segi waited in anticipation, wondering what the Iyaloja was up to.

'On the other hand, many in the kingdom see me as someone who is neither for nor against the royal family. Who believes that, after all, a market can prosper without a king to pay taxes to. Because they do not expect my loyalty to swing in any direction, they do not haunt me,' the Iyaloja said.

She paused before she added, 'As they do you.'

The Kingmakers stiffened, and so did Segi.

The Iyaloja closed her eyes, a small smile on her face as she considered her next words carefully. 'I am here because I cannot allow this to continue to those I consider very much like my sisters.'

The Kingmakers sighed in relief, and for the first time, the beginnings of smiles tugged their lips.

'So, I have found a way to re-instate you, to re-instate all of us into our role in the kingdom. And not allow us to continue to be pariahs.

'Even as the kingdom moves away from being ruled by a king.'

The Iyaloja turned to Segi.

'You know a certain ritual that I am sure was taught to you by the last Chief Kingmaker. The one where we invite the ancestors to stand before us and deliver us in our time of need.'

Segi looked towards the ground, considering the Iyaloja's words.

And the Iyaloja continued, 'This is definitely our time of need. The people have decided. And as we say, the voice of the people is the voice of God. But without sending the king home, the world will tear apart. Even now, we are running out of time.'

The Kingmakers nodded.

'We must summon the ancestors to help us seal that hole in the world. We might be able to convince them. And they will only listen to you, Segi – you are as much an ancestor as they are because you are the Chief Kingmaker, both alive and dead to this world,' the Iyaloja said.

'Please,' she continued. 'Summon them, help us plead with them. The people have decided, and there is no going back. Lead us, our Chief Kingmaker, as we transition into a new way. We do not have to suffer because we want better for our people.' Then the Iyaloja added cautiously, 'Neither do you, my sisters, you do not have to suffer.'

Segi sighed, thinking for several minutes as their eyes watched her face intensely. She promised to send word back about her decision before sunrise.

And now, weeks later, she gets up from the stone she sits on and walks up to the Iyaloja, nodding as she passes her. The other Kingmakers stop following as Segi walks deeper into the forest. Till no one can see her anymore. And the ritual begins.

~

It is hard to tell what happens to a kingdom – to any place – once it decides to be something else.

Segi calls upon the ancestors, their form like fluorescent light, glowing bright even in midday, and they agree to give the town another chance.

But no one knows what will happen; being given another chance does not mean success immediately. All of the celebrations of the town being delivered from doom are laced with uncertainty.

The day of the ritual, when Segi comes back from the forest unharmed, the people know they have been delivered. The town throws a party that lasts a week, but they are aware they have toyed with something vital about their home.

Many are relieved, but many more do not entirely know the way forward.

Segi, on the other hand, knows what will happen – a new divination appeared to her once the ancestors stitched the world back shut. And because of this, because she knows what will happen, she knows what she needs to do.

In the middle of the celebration, Segi slips away, back into the forest of the ancestors. Walks for hours before she sees the exact waterfall that had appeared in the divination. An oasis in a place that is otherwise almost a desert.

And she summons the king.

Not standing before him in spirit but in full flesh. Bringing to life the union they should have shared.

They stare at each other for a moment before she gestures to the waterfall and says to the king, 'You can go home now.'

With that, the king walks away into the rest of his life, and Segi does not die.

She knew she would not. The ancestors had changed things.

Segi has performed her last duty to the king, and she is no longer Chief Kingmaker. There is no longer a kingdom – or rather, a willing people – to make a king for.

And Segi stares at the waterfall for a moment, knowing she will one day walk under it too.

But she does not know whose arms will be waiting for her on the other side. The divination, detailed as it had been, did not reveal this.

BUSAYO AKINMOJU

Busayo Akinmoju is a writer. Her work has been published in *SmokeLong Quarterly*, *The Republic*, *A Coup of Owls*, *The Kalahari review*, among others. She likes to read, and to relax on long walks. You can check her website
https://busayomoji0.wixsite.com/a-busayo

THE CHANGELING OF SNEEM
Marianne Xenos

AFTER a long walk between worlds, the Dedanan group rested for the night. Four fairies, one human, and a small, winged beast gathered around a campfire. Their weaving route had taken a path from Boston in the Commonworld to an unnamed forest on the border of the Otherworld. Now they were tired and footsore, and they heated water for tea, passed containers of snacks, and made themselves comfortable. Joan, the only human present, grumbled – not for the first time – about too much walking and not enough magic. 'Can't you guys conjure up a flying carpet or a dragon?' The small, winged creature, Zilly, was actually a descendant of dragons and Simurghs. She looked at Joan pointedly and fluffed her wings.

Razi, a Dedanan bard with oak-brown skin, smiled and said, 'Just ask Zilly – dragons aren't pets, Joan. They don't serve at our whim. Though I wouldn't mind a nap on a soft woollen carpet, myself.'

The Dedanan took their name from the Celtic Tuatha de Danann, but they were a mixed group – with origins from Babylon to Belfast. They looked more like scruffy members of an eclectic rock band than fairies from a storybook. One, an urban fae with silver piercings and intricate skull tattoos, took a small brush out of his backpack and began untangling the knots of fur on Zilly's wings. He winked at Joan. 'If anybody's the pet, love, it's me, not the dragon.'

Razi was the troop's bard and storyteller, and as they settled in, someone asked him for a hearth story. Razi agreed as he finished braiding his long hair and shrugged out of his dusty leather jacket. Among the Dedanan, hearth stories required attention and formality. Trail stories could wander, teashop stories tolerated interruption, pillow stories often faded to dark, but hearth stories needed fire, a proper beginning and end, and uninterrupted attention from the listeners.

As the others settled in, Joan felt her worries stir. This journey was a search for her half-sister Lucie – young, rebellious and more than part-fae. She had disappeared twelve months ago, and all Commonworld clues were exhausted; Joan's best hope now was this Dedanan excursion to the Otherworld. The police assumed Lucie was a runaway, but Joan dreamed of her at night, crying on the far side of a yellow door or calling from beyond a crystal wall of water. Resting wasn't restful. She'd rather keep pushing, but they'd covered miles today, and unless Joan wanted to storm through the night exhausted and alone, she had to listen to her advisors. Right now, they advised a cup of tea, a hearth story, and a good night's rest. So, she pulled her knees to her chest and put her focus on Razi and the campfire.

Razi set a cup of tea to his left, rang a small silver bell, and waited until he had the group's attention to begin the formal benediction. 'There was one, there wasn't one, there was no one beside the light. And then and then again, between the darkness and the stars, begins our story.' He paused, and an expectant stillness fell over the group.

'This teller has loved many times,' Razi said, 'but only one marriage lasted longer than a thousand years. In other tales, I told you of my wife in Armenia and my husband in Tehran, but hear now the story of my life-love, Nessa, the Changeling of Sneem. The year was 560 A.D., more than a century after the coming of Patrick to Ireland.'

'But wait,' interrupted Joan. 'That was *before* the other two marriages. What do you mean by life-long? Who is she? Is she still alive?'

The group laughed and hushed her. Mearle, a Dedanan warrior with black feathers and beads tied into the tangle of her bright red hair, grabbed Joan's shoulders and whispered in a soft brogue, one that came and went with her moods. 'It's a hearth story, love. Interruptions are brutally punished.' Then she winked.

Razi smiled and shook his finger. 'Cultural relativity, Joan. Don't impose your human concepts of marriage, morality or storytelling on the Dedanan.'

The group quieted, and Razi began again.

'And so it was, many years ago, on the west coast of Ireland, a Sidhe-girl gave birth to an egg. This doesn't happen often, and the Dedanan still wonder how a Sidhe-girl survived mating with a bird deity, a Morrigan cousin, a god of battle and death. The bird god was wild as the north wind, barely corporeal and not in the least romantic. Their union was a one-night stand that lasted less than an hour, but the Sidhe-girl became pregnant, grew big, and eventually birthed an egg. She brooded the egg, not out of love but compelled by the spirit in the egg itself.

'For an egg, it was unnaturally bossy.'

A soft chuckle moved through the group, and Joan was perplexed, suspecting an inside joke. Mearle smiled and put a finger to her lips, and Razi continued.

'After days of dull brooding, the egg cracked open to reveal a fae-ish baby full of hunger and need. The Sidhe-girl was profoundly unsuited for motherhood and did one of the few compassionate acts of her flighty and flitful life. She dropped the child through an open window into a cradle that was, of course, already occupied. Changelings are usually exchanged, but the Sidhe-girl was done with babies. Like a cuckoo, she dropped her strong and hungry babe into the nest of a smaller and weaker child.

'The little fae chick, in the way of fairy tales, found herself in the home of a kindly couple. Changelings enchant their new parents, and when the mother found twin daughters in the crib that morning, she had two sets of memories. She knew she'd given birth to a single girl, but that memory was joined by another of birthing twins.

'The two babies, mortal and magical, were named Dar and Nessa, and like most true stories about children, things went very well until puberty.'

Rys, the leader of the Dedanan group and Razi's sister, was lean and muscular with spiky dark hair. She took the steaming kettle off the fire and poured water in silence. She smiled at Joan and raised the kettle to offer a refill, putting one finger over her lips for silence. Joan nodded and held out her cup.

'The circumstances were dangerous,' Razi continued, and Joan pulled her attention back to the story. 'Two daughters, one human and one of mixed-magical origin. As she reached puberty, Nessa, the changeling, glowed when angry and impulsively moved objects through the air. The air crackled, the shutters slammed, the milk soured. Many in Kerry held to the old ways, respecting the Gentry, as they called us. The true danger to the child was the new and determined presence of priests and the Church.

'Luckily, this humble bard had a mission in Ireland in the sixth century and found that the Sidhe were still buzzing with gossip about a wild Morrigan chick.'

A chuckle travelled around the campfire, and Joan again looked around the group, but nobody met her eye. If there was an inside joke, nobody was sharing.

'One day, as I walked near the banks of the Sneem River, I saw a flash of light over the nearby village. The signature was striking, fae-light intertwined with an elemental flare. But the light was childish, untrained magic, like a tantrum of flame, so I went to take a look.

'There, I found a girl of about thirteen years crying with rage while power crackled like lightning through her cloud of red hair.

'The girl's mother pleaded for quiet, but the child was incapable. She didn't control the power; the power controlled her. From a distance, I gentled and soothed, later slipped herbs and spells into their well water, and hoped the girl would survive. Every few weeks, I returned to spy on the unfortunate family. It didn't look like the parents could protect the wild chick much longer.

'Then, one day, from my hiding place on top of an ancient fairy fort that the locals avoided, I saw a young priest in a black cassock approach the house with an acolyte and a whip. The time had come, and I had to make my move, but first, I needed a few things.' Razi counted them off on his fingers, 'A cow, coins and a wedding ring. I only hoped the changeling could survive the night.'

Razi paused, and a clear ring from the silver bell broke the silence. Joan looked around in surprise and saw Rys, the group's leader, holding the bell. 'Dedanan point of order,' she said solemnly. 'I declare this a two-hearth story. Mearle will now join the hearth.'

Everybody except Joan broke into a raucous cheer and then quickly settled down.

'I still have my ring, love. Do you?' Mearle asked Razi, kissing him on the cheek. Everybody laughed except Joan, whose mouth fell open.

'No! Mearle? What?' Joan said.

'Look!' She showed the ring. 'Nessa Mearle Morrigan zal-Dedanan.'

Rys, the tough fairy warrior, laughed like a child enjoying an expected surprise. 'It's true! I was so pissed that he'd dragged some half-Morrigan teenager into our lives. The girl couldn't even control her glamour.'

'I still can't,' Mearle purred.

Razi took the silver bell from Rys, rang it again, and waited for silence. He said solemnly, 'Mearle has joined the hearth story.'

'This teller has loved many times,' said Mearle with a wink while the group chuckled.

'My sister-in-law will say my idea of a long-term relationship is staying for breakfast.' Now there was a full laugh. 'But this hearth story is about love, not romance, and we will honour love. I learned to love when my Sidhe-girl mother dropped me through an open window into my sister's nest. There is no deeper love than a twin, a sister, a comrade of the nursery. Without her, Nessa of Sneem would never have lived. When the bird inside my body tried to fly without wings, she grounded me. We learn to love in our nests, and it trains us for the work we do with our chosen families.'

Joan put her head on her knees and thought of Lucie. She and her sister weren't twins, but Mearle's words struck home. All her life, she'd felt like an outsider, and now, with these outsiders, she felt at home. The Dedanan were now part of her chosen family.

'Then and then again, between the darkness and the stars, I share my story.

'My father's name was Felim, and he had a gentle heart. He beat me once, and he cried as though he himself had been beaten. The priests said a demon, and not the wild natural gods, lived inside of me. So out of love – fearful and misguided love – he used his cane. Then he sobbed. I was a lucky changeling. My mother, Ailen, had a heavier hand, as Irish mothers often do, but she believed in the old gods and the Good Neighbours and had the sense to know that two things can be true at once. Yes, I was a changeling. And yes, I was her daughter. She never wavered.'

Mearle was normally loud and brash, and Joan had never heard her speak so long without cursing. Yet, despite the black leather and boots, and the mane of tangled red hair, Joan saw the child Nessa inside of Mearle for the first time. An ancient child.

'My parents protected me, but soon after my thirteenth birthday, when my moon cycle came, and my tantrums shook the stones of the church, the priest came to the door. Out in Kerry, they were still sceptical of priests, but the foreign religion, as some called the Church, was looking for traction, justification and power. People who were afraid of the Sidhe transferred their fear to the Church. Or they made a cowardly bargain and split their fears between the two.

'The priest was young and Roman, and he was overly interested in sinful girls and witches. His acolyte was a brute of a man known for his mistreatment of children. They banged on the door, and when my father opened it, the priest announced in a voice that carried through the village, "We've come about your daughter, Nessa. We must scourge the evil from her young flesh, Felim. She may be a witch."

'My mother looked him in the eye and said, "It's men like you brought the idea of evil and witches. There was a time we had respect for women and the old spirits."

'"Careful, Aileen," the priest growled, more like a hound than a man, "and think about both your daughters. I have the right to scourge them both."

'I pushed my sister behind me and glared at the priest. I would kill him before he touched my sister.

The priest had to take a step back to look up at me. I was only thirteen, but even then, I had the height of a Morrigan, although I didn't yet know the name.

'My mother put her hand on my shoulder, and I saw caution in her face and, more importantly, contempt for the priest, and it calmed me. She was nobody's fool.

'My mother looked at my father and nodded. Somehow, they would have a plan.

'The priest said, "Drop your dress, Nessa of Sneem, and prepare to meet the glory of God."'

The quiet of the hearth story was broken by a roar of protest from the Dedanan. One shouted something in Gaelic, and another agreed in Akkadian. Then Mearle held up one hand and rang the small silver bell for silence. She leaned forward, nodded and continued.

'Well, my mother grabbed the whip from the priest's hands, didn't she?' Mearle's brogue was swelling. '"Shame on you, Father," she scolded. "No man shall see her flesh except the Almighty God, and the beating will be from her Da's own hand. Wait outside and leave us to our shame."

'The priest went out the door, looking sorely disappointed, with his bully boy at his back. "I'll be listening!" the priest admonished. "And don't be lax, Felim. We demand blood as proof."

'My father nodded curtly at the priest and took the whip from my mother. When the door was closed, he said in a loud voice, "Nessa take off your dress." He handed the whip back to my mother and started taking off his own shirt. He gestured to the door with his head and pronounced theatrically. "This is for the sake of your eternal soul, daughter."

'My mother shook her head, confused, and the two stared at each other for a second in silence. Then, in the nature of a couple that ran a farm together for twenty years – raising chickens, cattle, babies and changelings – they nodded in agreement and got to work.

'My mother tried the whip on the chair, and my sister Dar began to cry. "How many?" my mother whispered.

'"How many lashes, Father?"

'"Twelve, and don't be a coward, man. Beat the demon from her flesh."

'My mother handed me a blanket and kissed both my cheeks. "Get on the floor, love, and scream for your life." Dar knelt beside me, sobbing. And we screamed like the ancient banshees while my mother whipped twelve bloody stripes on my father's back.

'"That's enough," shouted the priest. "Leave some flesh for tomorrow."

'"Get a rag," my father gasped. My mother understood and covered his back with a cloth, letting the blood soak through. Then she covered my naked back with the bloody rag and hid my father in the bedroom.

'The priest banged the door, swaggering in, suspicious. When he saw the blood, he was satisfied. "Where's Felim?"

'"Out back, throwing up. Where do you think?"

'"Well, the old coward did something right. I'll be back tomorrow. If she's not broken, I may not be able to hold back."

'As the door closed behind him, my mother made an ancient but obscene gesture at the priest's back. "These foreign priests enjoy their scourging. Did you see the bulge below his cassock?" I hadn't noticed, but I wasn't surprised.

'The next morning, when my mother was changing my father's bandages, we heard a loud knock at the door as a staff rang out upon the oak. A bold voice called, "Open the door for the Tuatha de Danaan."'

The group around the campfire broke into a loud cheer, and Joan jumped in her seat. Mearle laughed and handed Razi the bell. He let the laughter continue for a minute, then rang the bell again.

Razi waited with a smile, and the others settled down to listen.

'When I returned to the village, I came to the door dressed as a king, which in those days meant a sheep skin and a golden torque. I led a heifer on a rope and carried two bags of coins, one with silver and one with gold. I banged on the door with my wooden staff and introduced myself as Lugh Razilius of the Tuatha de Danaan.

'The mother took one hard look at me, then nodded her head, let me in and gave me the best chair. Christianity was a new thing in Ireland, but every peasant knew the Gentry.

'The father was obviously injured, but he said, "Would you take some food or drink?" And I said, "Only if you accept a favour in return."

'I drank the father's good mead, and we knew it had sealed our trust. The family had a claim on me now because among the Gentry – among all of the

Sidhe – accepting hospitality, especially the best honey mead, is a binding contract.

'I explained that Nessa was a child of the Sidhe and one of the more ancient gods. They weren't surprised, and they looked relieved. The other daughter, Dar, asked, "Have you come for her, then?" And when I said yes, she burst into tears.

'Nessa came in from the backyard. She was a fabulous monster – red and gold and fizzing with magic. The sister introduced me as Lugh Razilius of the Tuatha de Danaan, and Nessa looked at me and snorted in disbelief. Dar told Nessa to look more closely, which she did, and her eyes went wide. She'd never seen Dedanan before, but she recognized me as kin, even if our ties were distant.

'I brought out my ring, stood before her, and clasped my hands in a humble but carefully practised manner. "Nessa, I want you to be my bride."

'She curled her lip and sneered, so I continued with my practised oath. "I promise to share power and mastery in both battle and magic, to celebrate all of your loves and desires, and to touch you only when you wish to be touched, so long as the stars may rule."

'Then I paused. "More practically, if we marry, your entire family will be protected by the Dedanan. The priest means you harm, and he will punish your family as well for resisting."

'She bit her lip and scowled.

'"What about my sister, Dar? Can she come with us?"

'"She's human and can't come." Dar looked both devastated and relieved.

'"Okay," Nessa said. In a time of arranged marriages, it was a decent arrangement. "But I promise nothing in return," she said. And I agreed.

'The father called back the priest and had us married immediately. Despite the odd and un-Christian match of Dedanan Prince and Morrigan Changeling, everyone was happy. Thirteen was a marriageable age for girls in ancient Ireland, but I offered a long, long engagement at Queen Maeve's palace in Connaught. The parents received the heifer and a bag of gold, and the priest got thirty pieces of silver. If the man understood the irony, he still took the silver.

'You've heard my vows, and as she accepted the ring, Nessa promised nothing. Certainly not to love, honour and obey. To this day, we've kept our vows, and as the old-timers say: The tale has been finished, but the crow has not yet arrived at his house.'

Razi rang the bell, and the group was quiet for a moment, obviously happy with the story.

Joan raised her hand timidly, 'Can I ask a question now?'

Mearle said, 'Joan would like to know if we're still married and if we ever had sex. And if so, was it good? Or was it like kissing the family dog? Would you like to answer?'

'No,' Joan interrupted. 'I want to know about the sister.'

Mearle smiled. 'Dar lived happily. She joined the convent in Kildare, where all the smart girls went, and fell in love with another nun.'

Joan felt relieved and happy for Dar, but when Mearle sat beside Joan and put her arm around her,

Joan found herself crying. Mearle guessed the reason.

'We'll find her, love. We'll bring your sister home.'

Razi came and sat with them, and one by one, the rest of the group huddled close. Zilly, who had flown into a nearby tree in preparation for her night-time hunt, rumbled in sympathy over their heads.

Mearle pulled a short dagger from her boot and said, 'When I feel overwhelmed, Joan, I sharpen my talons. Before we tuck you into bed tonight, let us teach you some Morrigan moves.' The group pulled Joan to her feet, and for the next twenty minutes, the dark glade filled with grunts, laughter, and the flash of fairy metal in firelight. The dragon postponed her hunt to swoop around their heads and hoot encouragement while Mearle taught Joan to fight like a Dedanan.

MARIANNE XENOS

Marianne Xenos is writer and visual artist living in western Massachusetts. Along with narratives about shapeshifters and urban dragons, Marianne is working on a fantasy novel set in Boston's queer community in 1983. Two years ago she shifted her focus from visual art to speculative fiction, and published her first short story in 2022.
www.mariannexenos.com

STRAWBERRY HEARTS
Corinne Pollard

IT was their first summer left unattended, and Alma was worried. She peered down from her bedroom window, inspecting the unruly strawberry patch. Their untamed runners were thriving under the June sky, but April had prolonged its showers. The wetness had invited a predator: a halo of mould had begun to mummify the fruit.

Alma knew it was a matter of time before the rest were infected. There was nothing she could do. She used to be a methodical gardener; if there was a problem, she solved it. Now she was a watcher.

Her fingertips rubbed together; the earth's grainy softness flickered through her mind. When was the last time she had submerged her hands beneath the soil and felt a plant's fragile life? How she ached to crawl through dirt, breathe in fruity sweetness and lick crimson juices.

'Mistress Stern?' A mouse-like voice echoed from the open doorway.

Alma sighed before turning to spy Harold, a skeleton of a boy, dressed in soot. His charcoal hair had grown long enough to curtain his forehead and droop into his tiny eyes; his frequent habit of swiping at it had failed to stop the strands tangling into his long eyelashes. Pyjamas hung upon his small, tree-like frame, their threads hovering in an invisible breeze.

The nine-year-old fidgeted, unable to cross the threshold, unable to meet Alma's piercing gaze, and unable to use his fringe as a shield.

'What is it?' Alma crossed her arms. Her nightgown crinkled like tissue paper.

Harold swallowed, licked his shrivelled lips, and coughed. 'I'm hungry. Do you… have anything to eat?'

'You are always hungry, and you will remain hungry.'

Harold gulped and lowered his head. 'Please, just a bit of bread?'

Alma's patience snapped.

She scowled and glided, in the blink of an eye, to loom over him. Her white nightgown flashed, billowing. Her long dark hair blew up and outwards like a stretched spiderweb seeking prey. The natural beauty of her fine skin was overshadowed by how tense and fierce her gaze was.

Squeaks escaped Harold's trembling mouth. It was finally enough to hurtle him back down the dusty corridor. He left no footprints.

'You should be nicer to Harold, Miss Stern,' Edna announced with her head poking out of the opposite bedroom. The door was shut.

'Mind your manners, Edna. It's Mistress Stern.'

Click-click. Edna's head rotated. The door's wood limited her wispy neck.

'Manners are no longer important.' Edna grinned as her chestnut eyes glittered with unsaid understanding.

Alma crossed her arms again. 'If you have something to say, Edna, then come out.'

The head was sucked through the door. A couple of seconds passed before it unlocked with a rickety swing.

The twelve-year-old's ruby shoes clopped upon the blackened floorboards. She sashayed, clumsily mimicking her Hollywood idols. Her creamy pigtails and chequered ribbons swayed with her exaggerated hips along the catwalk.

Edna's grin remained wide as Alma eyed her sky-blue dress with a frown.

'Stop dressing up as Dorothy, Edna.'

'Well, when I've managed to work out how to alter one's appearance, I'll add stockings.'

Alma's frown deepened, cracking into hardened wrinkles. 'I keep hearing scratches on our joining wall. You'd better not be defiling the wallpaper again!'

'The wallpaper? You're still worried about the wallpaper?!' Edna giggled.

Alma pushed past the giddy child to circle the empty bedroom. Edna's room was smaller, with faded, floral walls that were ripping at the corners.

'Stop messing around! This is not a game. When Mr Woolner returns…' said Alma, while biting her lip.

'Mr Woolner survived.' Edna's cheekbones deflated. Her lips thinned, and her lively eyes narrowed.

'What do you mean?'

'My eyes are open, Harold's are closed, but you…' Edna lifted her face to stare at her elder. 'You must stop existing with only one of your eyes closed.'

'And you need to stop defiling the wall!' Alma shrieked as she spotted the markings.

They were etched deep with blooms of paper splinters. The wallflowers were chopped off.

Alma wagged a firm finger, scolding Edna.

'Of course, you'd notice my calendar scratches, but not the burnt-up rug or the scorched curtains,' Edna muttered as Alma exited.

Alma returned to her usual spot.

How she admired the strength of her berries as they battled against harsh glacial crystals. The flurry was thickening. It shrouded the tangled vines and buried the crimson skin. Only their leafy heads poked out.

The blizzard blurred the window view. Beyond it, there was a gravel road that twisted between grass-trimmed slopes. In the furthest distance, a woodland towered with out-of-control branches. Yet the blizzard hid all. The snow clouds pelted down with no end in sight.

Alma bit her lip. Her berries had to survive this.

'Still on the lookout?' Edna drifted to her side. She tilted her head, peering through the glass to admire the blizzard's efforts.

'Aren't you cold?' Alma asked, eyeing Edna's dress.

'No. Not cold, just tired,' Edna sighed. 'Aren't you cold?'

Alma tensed. 'A little.'

'Liar.'

Alma did not argue. There was fatigue upon Edna's youthful face she had never seen before. Gone were the sparkles in her chestnut eyes. Gone were the blooming roses upon her cheeks. Gone were the magical dimples when she smiled. Wrinkles were settling under her eyelashes, at the top of her nose and forehead. Paleness was invading as if the outside blizzard was also stripping Edna of colour.

'Do you think this weather will stop anytime soon?' Edna asked.

Alma shrugged.

Edna continued as if to convince herself. 'There has to be an end. This can't be all it is. Forever fixed.'

'What are you talking about? Nothing's fixed,' said Alma sharply. 'You were once a scared little girl clutching her teddy bear. Now, you're a teenager. An annoying teenager.'

'We have quite a history,' Edna agreed. 'Do you ever miss home?'

'No. It was no longer home.'

The wind blew through the glass with a moan, and the pair paused to listen. Its chilling voice cried out as the snow piled higher.

'I just hope that with no end in sight, we don't end ourselves instead,' Edna whispered.

Alma's throat dried up.

Edna's gaze was fixed on the outside, dismissing the chaos. Her deep thoughts carried her off somewhere, and Alma did not dare ask about it. Edna's eyes had darkened. With her pale skin, she cast an eerie likeness to a corpse, sending shivers down Alma's back.

'Time is flying by,' Edna murmured, spinning on her heel to leave.

'...I have a bit of bread, please?' Harold's squeaky voice whimpered. Alma blinked down at him from her doorway.

A glance over her shoulder revealed sunlight bathing the room. She exhaled. Maybe her berries survived after all.

'Wait, wasn't it just snowing?'

Harold cocked his head. 'No, Mistress. There has been a lot of rain.'

'No, it was snowing. There was a storm.'

Alma hurried to her spot. Small leaves fanned out in the dirt. They were alive, but her relief was short-lived.

'No!' she gasped. The predator had swarmed more of her berries. It was spreading fast and draining them. The ripened curves now squelched black ooze.

'Mistress, about the bread…'

'I do not care about your stupid bread, Harold. Go and annoy Edna.'

Harold lowered his soot-smeared face, struggling to suppress his tears. Droplets leaked upon his razor-sharp cheekbones.

Alma paid no attention. She cursed the house's barrier for the thousandth time; if only it would let her pass and attend to her patch. Her bare foot tapped upon the creaky floorboards with each tick of an invisible clock inside her mind.

A headache prickled but did not erupt, the pain dialling down enough to vanish as if she had imagined it. Alma wished the pain in her heart would fade away too. Each scan of every leaf, root, stalk, and fruit throbbed.

Then her eagle eyes detected a problem. She double-checked, triple-checked. She wished her sight was tricking her, but there was no mistake.

A fruit was missing.

She gnawed on her thumbnail as a fever surged. It scalded through her veins and then burst forth. The bedroom door flew off its hinges, landing flat in the corridor where her main suspect attempted to flee.

'Vere is it?!' Alma shrieked. She grabbed Harold's thin shoulder and pushed him to the side.

Harold shrank. 'I haven't done anything! Please, Mistress, you're hurting me.'

'Vere is mein schtravperry?'

'Strawberry?'

'Ja, vu hungradeful child! Vu sdole it, didn't vu?'

'That's enough, Alma.' Edna strode in with her pigtails swaying sideways.

'Don't tell me vat to do, Edna!'

'No one has your strawberry. Now let him go.'

Alma tightened her grip, hard enough for Harold to whimper. 'One of vu has it. Giffe it pack, pefore I hinfolffe Mr Voolner.'

'I don't have it!' Harold wailed as memories of Mr Woolner striking his bottom dashed through his screaming mind.

'Even if you had it, you couldn't eat it, Alma. What would you do with it then?' Edna levitated closer. 'Open your eyes, Alma. Food would be a waste on you.'

'How dare vu!'

'Please let go! I won't ask for bread anymore.'

Silence fell as the two women glared at each other. Forgotten but caught in the crossfire, Harold dangled from Alma's claw, struggling. He grabbed her arm and tried to shove her with all of his strength.

Alma's nails dug in, and Harold blubbered, certain that Alma had drawn blood. It flowed as his body froze.

Alma spied on him with her peripheral vision. His cries penetrated her raging haze. His futile attempts for freedom amused her.

From Harold's chest, something glowed.

Hypnotised, Alma stared and pulled Harold closer. She knew it. She knew he had stolen her strawberry. There it was, glowing with plump curves, shaped like a love heart, ready for plucking.

'Are you listening to me? Let Harold go!'

Edna's shrills were ignored.

Harold flinched as Alma's other hand seized his dusty pyjama top, and before he realised the danger, she raised the flimsy material. Her fist plunged inside.

Sticky ooze surrounding her precious berry congealed as a barrier. It was like her hand was swimming through gelatine. An aroma of salty, metallic fluid flowed. Alma shovelled and tossed the gelatine aside.

Edna's shrills gained volume. Alma's arm throbbed as smaller fists punched her, but Alma did not care.

Her palm cupped her prize. It hung, slathered in thick gelatine, beating a rhythm to her desire. She was puzzled to find it connected to many stalks, but this did not deter her. Her mouth watered as her fingers made quick, expert work, picking with rotating twists and then plucking it.

She could not wait any longer. Her first bite devoured a red flood; each sugar wave tingled her taste buds. Moaning with pleasure, she sucked at the berry's flesh until her mouth wore lipstick. A sickly caramel odour fragranced the air, prickling her nostrils. Another bite embedded bumpy seeds between her teeth. Sweet juices sickened to a sour tang. Her tongue licked every drop. The last bite was swallowed ardently, seeping a glow along her throat to the pit of her stomach.

Satisfied, Alma left.

Edna stared after her, dumbstruck. She panted hard, seeking air; it eluded her. Though the air was not necessary, she became desperate. It was like her throat had been sewn closed.

Her knees bent. She let herself collapse. The black wood creaked under her in protest.

At that moment, she felt human. Weak. Insignificant.

Harold had been whimpering moments ago. Now, silent dust floated, the specks reflecting in the sunlight. His disappearance seemed impossible, but Edna had watched in the front row of the horror show. It was undeniable.

She willed herself to stop shaking. Her body didn't listen.

Why couldn't I have done more? Harold didn't deserve this. I have failed him. The guilt dropped on her shoulders like a ton of rocks.

Time passed. Tears flowed.

I need to do something now. I owe it to him.

Her quivering hands curled. She raised herself by her white-tipped knuckles. Gritting her teeth, she drifted to Alma's lair without any plan. She knew she was outmatched in strength and height.

With a hallucinating mind, Alma had become a danger Edna hadn't foreseen. An unpredictable force born from immortality.

The bedroom door was untouched and the entrance vacant. The doorway hinges had rusted to a coffee brown and gaped at Edna as she edged past. The large window announced bedtime; darkness had descended. It was a blank, stygian canvas; sunless, starless, and moonless. It swallowed the land, allowing only glimpses of the darkest trees.

Alma's curves in her nightgown of pearl were as clear as daylight. Edna could even see the worn-out ribbon and the wavy lace trimmings. Alma's dark locks wrapped around the lace collar as she twiddled with one. The invisible breeze flew them across her neck like a lacerating slash.

Edna shivered without thinking.

Alma peered at her night-time view, brooding with pursed lips. 'I remember the fire now,' she declared out of the blue.

Edna's mouth dropped before she cleared her throat. 'It was an accident.'

Alma shook her head. 'It was me.'

'What?'

'Mr Woolner found another lover. He was finished with me.'

Edna looked away.

'Edna, it was my decision. I intended to ensure our safety by any means necessary. I don't blame you or Harold.'

'It was blackmail, and we should've run.'

Seething rage raced across Alma's face. 'Run where? Back home? No, it was my decision. I accepted being his lover all those years, and he kept his word. We were safe. He didn't tell them where we were.'

'He found another.'

Alma frowned. 'Yes, and he said he would tell. Our deal was off.'

'The fire?' Edna pressed.

'We fought, and I smashed the menorah. He fled. The coward.'

'You didn't warn us.' Edna's lip trembled. 'Why didn't you find us? Why didn't you give us the chance to escape?'

Alma swallowed. 'I decided we were better off dead than in their hands.'

'You don't get to decide that,' Edna whispered as a tear crawled down her cheek. 'You are no better than them. This netherworld has only been bearable because of the two of you. Then you erased Harold.'

'He stole from me.'

'He didn't steal! He was a good soul. Besides, you're already dead! Why are you so obsessed with those damn strawberries?!'

'Without them, I have nothing. Without them, Mr Woolner won't…' Alma clenched her jaw.

Edna balled her hands into fists. 'You're messed up. Mr Woolner did not love you.'

'Shut up!' Alma yelled.

Edna ignored her. She was past the point of caring. More tears sprinkled, unnoticed. 'You killed us! You're a monster! You ate Harold's soul, core, heart, essence, whatever you call it! He isn't here anymore because of you.'

'I ate my strawberry.' Alma strode closer with a darkening tone. 'You have one too. One of my strawberries.'

'What? Are you going to eat me too?' A hysterical giggle escaped.

'You have my strawberry.' Alma's shadowed eyes glazed over. They shone like a ceramic coating.

'Stop now, Alma. I do not want to be driven into a corner.'

'Give me my strawberry.' Alma held out a hand.

'Your strawberries are dead! We have been here for years! The house is falling apart, and no one comes. I am not even sure what year it is anymore. I'm not sure if the war is over or if Mr Woolner is alive. Please, Alma!'

Her words triggered no reaction. Alma's palm hovered inches away, with Harold's spectral remains lingering under her fingernails. The metallic aroma penetrated Edna's senses. It was a wake-up call; talking was no longer an option. Edna breathed out and focused on letting go. She was light as a feather. She glided into a descent.

Alma scowled and spat out rude words in German.

Edna grinned, but once covered from view, the grin fell off her face. She drifted sideways and rose to peek, breathing into the floorboards, inhaling the musky dampness.

She had managed to drift behind Alma, and as her guardian cursed at the fire-scorched floor, Edna knew she couldn't hide forever. She needed to fight. Like she had practised many times, she sailed back. Before Alma could sense her, and with no hesitation, she sank her fist through Alma's spine and inside her ribcage.

Alma gasped and then shrieked. She tried to pull herself out of Edna's reach, but Edna held on. Fluids leaked down her arm as her hand clutched at what she guessed was Alma's spectral heart. Alma's nightgown stained in an instant, its pearl-white cloth darkening. The red waterfall splashed and puddled under their feet as Alma struggled in vain.

Edna held on as her smaller spectral body was tossed around with each jolting spin. Her tiny feet flew in every direction, losing each of her ruby shoes. Again and again, she slammed against Alma's back. It was a bizarre dance to the death.

The heart squelched in Edna's palm as she tried to yank it out. It refused to budge. More blood gushed. On the eighth nauseating spin, Edna realised she needed a different tactic. Fluids flowed into her mouth. Edna spluttered while blindly twisting and ripping one vein and artery at a time. Motion sickness threatened as she thumbed the last velvet-soft connection. The monstrous situation sank in, and sweat dribbled as her heartbeat increased.

No, I can't do it. Her grip loosened for a second. *Harold's pleading words. His hopeful eyes. His sooty pyjamas. All of him is lost. There is no point.*

'I will have my strawberries!' Alma howled as her hair swung anticlockwise.

Edna was flung off.

Alma's mouth twisted a victory grin as saliva escaped down her chin. She reached behind to feel inside the gaping hole, but no matter how hard she patted inside, she couldn't find it. Her body was empty.

Edna had plucked it.

It beat in her palm, and transfixed, she stared at it.

There is no point except my survival.

Decision made, she brought the glowing heart to her blood-stained lips. She widened her jaw and struck.

It tasted like sickly berries. Numbness invaded Edna's mind as a raspberry tang pricked her tongue. She swallowed, wanting more. Her desire overtook all her senses – even the icy stabs of loneliness. She had feared being alone, but nothing else mattered now. The raspberry heart was devoured.

CORINNE POLLARD

Corinne Pollard is a disabled writer from West Yorkshire, UK, published in *Sirens Call*, *Black Hare Press*, *Three Cousins Publishing*, *Trembling with Fear, World of Myth*, and *Paragraph Planet*. Also, Corinne is co-editor for the Yorkshire anthology *Aire Reflections* with her dark stories and poetry inside. With a degree in English Lit and Creative Writing, Corinne has always enjoyed the world of dark fantasy. Aside from writing, Corinne enjoys metal music, visiting graveyards, and shopping for books to read. Follow her dark world on Twitter and Instagram: @CorinnePWriter

MITOSIS
Samir Sirk Morató

HE doesn't want a birthday party because of The Men, the ones who stalk him and try to poison his food, but his foster mother would be upset – perhaps enough to return him – so Necalli stays silent. He peels another cuticle off; the elastic to his birthday hat cuts his chin. Wind rustles through their strip of lawn.

'Don't worry, Necalli.' Shannon shoves napkins beneath a sweaty lemonade pitcher. 'I'm sure your classmates are just late.'

Necalli nods. He watches their fence line. The picnic table is close enough for someone to fling arsenic pellets onto the sheet cake and into the plastic cups. They've tried it before. They'll try again. He wants to tell Shannon that no one will show because everyone thinks he's a fucking loser, but some people pocketed his invitations instead of trashing them, and The Men are prowling. Explanation isn't important.

His gut knots when a stranger plods by the fence. Distant car brakes scream. Time slithers forward in terrible, twisting ways. Shannon repeats excuses as twilight contaminates the deserted party, turning the dripping tablecloth and buttercream to visceral sludge. Necalli relaxes when she finally removes the cake before he registers the mothy darkness. The desolation.

'I'm sorry, Necalli.' Shannon fidgets. 'Maybe people got caught up in other plans. It's a busy time of year.'

'Spring break starts Monday,' Necalli says. 'They're not busy.'

'Maybe spring break is why they're busy. Scheduling is hard!'

Shannon talks to him as if he isn't nicknamed Bonebag at school for his sunken eyes and his billion vitamins or wasn't arrested for battery before she acquired him. Necalli's nausea rises. His loneliness chokes him; his heartbeat clogs his lungs. He flees inside, Shannon cringing on the lawn. A slurry of panic floods his throat. Stairs scream beneath his feet. Necalli sprints into the bathroom. The door slams behind him, locking, as he retches water into the toilet. The adrenaline and relief of purging course through him. He fits inside himself again.

Necalli realises something is different when his entrails follow their contents.

The intestines come first. The charnel. Coil after coil worms from Necalli's mouth, splashing into the bowl. He cannot tell if this is real. His inability to breathe is. He heaves, tears streaking his face, when hydrochloric acid sears his oesophagus. His stomach balloons from his mouth, a sloppy pink sandbag, kidneys riding on its arc, a greenish gallbladder clinging to its tail. Necalli's sobs drown in the river of flesh forcing itself past his teeth, then vanish when his lungs bloom from his lips, inflating and deflating frantically, a liver barrelling out behind them. Necalli almost collapses while expelling it all. Ropes of drool untether from his teeth as he pukes a pulsating heart, escorted by webs of vein.

He stares at the organ heap overflowing from the toilet while his fingers grip the porcelain, the bathroom fan roaring, his mind silent.

~

Flushing won't work (Necalli tries it before he realises the toilet's flooding; he fishes the organs out in panic). Trashing them isn't an option either (Shannon will find the organs. What will she think or say?). Necalli hides them in the tub before scrubbing the toilet. Then he seals them in a turkey oven bag and secretes them in his room. Shannon bids him goodnight not long after, promising him better futures. Her smudged eyeliner renders her eyes lopsided and hollow.

Necalli restrains his screams while her rambling puts him on pins and needles. Can she hear the entrails sloshing? Can she smell copper on his breath? When Shannon catches him tearing off another cuticle, she embraces him. The way she sugar-coats situations and rubs his back flusters Necalli. He's no prize. He isn't a toddler, or a rescue dog, or a renovation project either. But he's too distracted to be humiliated. Necalli eats comforts from her palm the way Shannon wants him to, then vibrates beneath his covers until she leaves.

He sprints to his closet and peeks in. He starts. The organs are throbbing. Necalli sees his heart beating against the bag, spraying blood with every squeeze. The heat emitting from the offal pile fogs the closet.

What can he do but lay on the floor? Necalli stares at the plastic stars on his ceiling. He checks his wrist. It's warm; it's still. Necalli pats every inch of his body, flexes his limbs, and yanks on his tongue. He breathes in seesawing tandem with the organs' throbbing, then faster, then faster before he catches himself. Necalli buries a tooth in his lip. A whine slips free.

If this is unreal, purging will help. If it is real, purging might unmake him. What if he turns inside out and ends up in the toilet? What if his skeleton crawls free? Necalli presses on his belly. He watches his skin sink in until it catches, like a stretched trampoline, right above his spine. His muscles quiver. So this is real. Necalli removes his hand, relieved. His belly squelches before resuming its shape.

Everyone else perceives reality differently than he does. Despite his terror, he took a hammer to The Man invading his last foster home because he *knew* That Man aimed to grind poison into the baby formula (he'd never had a sister before, much less lost one), only for the family to insist The Man was a plumber, and Necalli was a monster. They returned him not a week after to protect the baby he'd acted for. As if he'd ever touch her. That memory chews at Necalli in lieu of stomach acid. Maybe he's been empty since then. He's always punished for defending himself. He's always wrong.

The heart gushes. Necalli, hypnotised, marinating in abandonment, watches his lungs steam beneath it. Even his organs have left him. He sprints downstairs for a garbage bag at midnight when he hears blood groaning against its confines.

Somehow, the organs are expanding. Developing. Necalli sleeplessly watches fat marble their gaps before nets of muscle pulse out around them. He loses sight of the action at 3:00 am when he ties the garbage bag shut in fear. He hears blood gush free as something sharp punctures the turkey bag. Then wet squirming. Wheezing. A hematoma amasses in the bag, expanding its sides with every crawling minute. Feverish heat clenches the bedroom. Pours sweat into Necalli's vacant body. At some point, he turns sixteen. That means little while raw creation is happening before him.

It's predawn when fingers work through the plastic. Necalli, sitting on the carpet, stares as a bloody, off-kilter copy of himself crowns from the bag's slit. It's him, wiped an inch to the left before the ink finished drying. Him with the blur of dirty glass built into his flesh. Neither a sibling nor a double, but some third, terrible thing. When their gazes meet, Necalli knows this not-him is empty of anything but instinct. It's a crawling system of tubes and fluids, aware that it must replenish itself. Nothing more.

He lifts his hand. Not-him stares. *Raise your hand,* Necalli demands. He feels the order shoot not through his vocal cords but his synapses. Instead of ending in him, it leaps to his organs. Not-him mirrors Necalli. Untouching, palms parallel, they sit in the murk, glistening with blood and sweat: imperfect reflections beneath fake stars. Necalli, lungless, cannot gasp. Not-him's presence is a burning dot in his mind. A pin on a map.

Prove you're real, Necalli says.

Not-him laces their fingers, brings Necalli's pinkie to his lips, then rips its jagged cuticle off with his teeth. Necalli's finger reddens in a burst of pain. Relief overwhelms him. He watches his skin disappear between not-him's perfect incisors. (That mouth contains only incisors.) For once, he's right. No other reality hides behind a gameshow door. Necalli squeezes his wet pinkie in reassurance even as he wills not-him to shower and leave.

Gossamer threads stretch between them as Necalli's replica disappears into the streets. The dot in Necalli's mind moves several spaces. Shivering as he disposes of the bloody bags in a dumpster, he looks at not-him's footprints in the frost. It doesn't feel like not-him ever departed. Necalli is alone; he is no longer singular. He cries.

Unlike parents, classmates, or his mind, whatever he made will be with him until they're destroyed.

~

It can't be The Men's doing if it comes from himself.

'You're voracious!' Shannon ruffles Necalli's hair while she serves him a fifth plate of pancakes sans vitamins. 'Goodness, where does it all go?'

Necalli, plumper than he's ever been, shrugs. Shannon trembles in pride as she watches him gather his books. Summer's death rattle gasps at their windows. Shannon counts the remaining garbage bags and searches for the missing cleaner again while Necalli organises his backpack. Her helplessness endears her to Necalli. Without him, she'd die of ignorance. He awkwardly hugs her – how strange, to feel another's affectionate body against his – before he leaves for his bus stop. She deserves pity. He deserves touch.

Outside, clumps of scarlet leaves hang overhead: the first bruises in the canopy. Cracks lace the sidewalk beneath Necalli's sneakers like lightning scars. Chill isn't here yet. It is coming. The world inhales before death.

'Say hi to your friends for me!' Shannon calls from the kitchen.

Friends! Necalli ugly-laughs.

'I will, Mom,' he shouts.

Paranoia strikes three blocks away. Maybe The Men are following him. Maybe they're seeking opportunities to powder his lunchbox with anthrax or to smear cyanide on his sandwich. If they can't do it on the bus, they'll try it at school. Necalli halts. Breathes deeply. Closes his eyes. He reaches into the veins webbing his eyelids, then launches a *hello!* into his depths. Several fever-hot presences call back: *hello, hello, hello!* Necalli feels their proximities. Four are far, two are a park away, and one is nearby. His regrowing organs twinge.

If Necalli gorges, he can puke his guts into a new companion every month. It's getting easier. The fleshfriends are growing faster. Necalli's misprinted copies of himself leave the tub seconds after realisation. Walk and talk and everything. Like baby dolls.

He calls to the closest dot. *Come here! Follow me!* Then he grinds his teeth, pretending he's commanded nothing. If he admits what he's doing, the paranoia wins. Necalli waits with his back against a sign while a boiling speck of neurons draws closer and closer on his radar. He ceases fidgeting when a familiar silhouette rounds the corner two blocks down.

He sighs. His shoulders loosen. Of course he's being followed. It's just a fleshfriend. Not a Man. He's safe. Necalli resumes walking.

(He cannot see his face in the fleshfriends' unless he squints. They have his features, but the flow of those features always differs. The second fleshfriend has nothing but index fingers; the fifth's eyes are inverted. So on and so forth. Necalli loves them all. Though they linger in gutters and beneath bridges until they're called, they're always present. Most viscera operate unseen.)

Sunshine heats Necalli's face. Leaves crunch beneath his boots. How beautiful those sensations are when they don't signify that someone could hunt him. How fucking wonderful it is to exist without punishment. Necalli pays his bus fare without fearing those in line behind him. The fourth person waiting isn't a person. Necalli hums when it sneaks on the bus. His cells sing.

He commutes alone. He'll remain alone at school too. That sting is bearable. Necalli's mind never ceases churning with subcutaneous truths, never ceases haemorrhaging conspiracies, yet he's discovered a method to keep them staunched. Necalli spies his fleshfriend's reflection in the bus window. It's the first replica. He, too, is sixteen. His hair is greasy, his stolen sweater crooked, his lips parted in an approximation of joy. A pigeon distracts him; his pupils shift. His gaze leaves Necalli for a moment. Their eyes pretend to meet in the glass. Necalli smiles.

A middle-aged woman studies them from her seat, brows knit in confusion. She points at Necalli. Authority seeps from her pores.

'Young man,' she says, 'you should sit with your brother.'

Necalli studies his healed cuticles. 'You're mistaken, ma'am. That's a stranger.'

The woman's expression clouds with uncertainty. Doubt. Necalli glows with vicious glee as he gestures at the fleshfriend.

'We're not related at all,' he says.

SAMIR SIRK MORATÓ

Samir Sirk Morató is a scientist, artist, and flesh heap. Some of their work can be found in *body fluids*, *Carmen Et Error*, *Rejection Letters, Somos En Escrito*, and *Runebear Weekly*. They are on Twitter and Instagram as @spicycloaca.

MERMAID TAILS AND TINFOIL HATS
Anastasia Jill

FIRST, they take my shoelaces, bra, underwear and belt. Next are accessories: my Star of David pendant, plastic rings, sterling silver hoop earrings. They even take the tampon between my legs.

'A crafty patient can turn it into a weapon,' the orderly tells me. 'It's standard for the Baker Act. No need to worry.'

But I am full of worry, doesn't he understand? I am naked and pallid as a beam of light. A man watches me through plexiglass from behind a pair of thick bifocals, the glass jaundiced from years of manic cigarette smoking. There are men everywhere – even the nurses have intrusive man-eyes.

'Can I use the bathroom?' I say.

No. If I need to pee, they will give me a cup.

My belongings are placed in a big plastic bag. All I can think is how bad it is for the environment. I am given a neon-green gown. A nurse commands, 'Put it on.' I do so in front of the whole behavioural health unit. My backside is exposed as there are no ties. It flows behind me like a polypropylene tail as I am led into a room locked from the outside.

No windows.

No blankets.

Just a bed and an eight-by-twelve space.

I slam my head against the wall, an old nervous trait I haven't engaged in since I was fifteen years old. A few hard slams, and I am out. When I come to, no one has noticed. I stay on the floor with my eight-ball-black eyes and spinning head.

I stare at the ceiling, counting tiles to pass time. The indents look like seashells peppering the roof. At some point, the staff psychiatrist comes into the room. She is a slender woman with drooping eyes and orange scrubs. She regards the gaping wound on my arm and asks me two questions.

'Thoughts of hurting yourself?'

'No.'

'Thoughts of harming anyone else?'

'No.'

She tuts once, twice, says, 'I know you're lying.' She writes something on a chart and leaves me all alone. Later that night – perhaps the next morning – I am transported from the country hospital to a psychiatric ward, though the EMTs call it a 'treatment facility' in chipper, preschool voices.

The facility in question is a dense forest of crumbling green buildings. Patients freely walk from doors that swing like loose baby teeth. Inside, the walls are white, and intake nurses sit behind bulletproof glass. The floor is the colour of frothy phlegm, and fluorescent lights are spotted with dead bugs.

The staff talk amongst themselves, all about me. A secretary's lips move like pink beta fish behind the glass, transcribing me into numbers: *Twenty-one-year-old female, 5'4, 140 lbs, 5150, suspected manic depression, toxicology positive for blah, blah, yada, yada, who cares...* They describe me as hostile, resistant, as per the emergency room notes. I am none of those things, but it's in print, so it's decided.

'I can hear you,' I spit out. Actual saliva follows. 'I'm standing right here.'

They ignore me. I fold like paper while they finish the evaluation. I'm sorted into a wheelchair, then pulled and prodded into a seafoam hallway.

An aquarium of grief – mammals behind glass and doctors like fish flopping in and out of hazy blue doors. A line forms outside a smoky room; the cafeteria, I presume. I catch the gaze of a young woman with flaxen hair. Her honeyed eyes are sad, knuckles pinched tight around a mermaid doll.

She is like me, a girl lost in this aseptic, manic sea.

~

Dr Maxine is my appointed counsellor. Sequin-pink lipstick poorly masks her flared teeth. Her smile is comforting as an embrace as she says, 'I'm going to do everything I can to help you.'

I barely listen, glancing around her office. There are binders stuffed with files, bright pink post-it notes. Posters for various medications hang from drab, grey frames. On her desk is a picture of her, arms wrapped around a man's waist, her russet bust glowing under the shape of a mango-coloured bathing suit. A dog sits at her feet, wide-jawed and cheery-eyed.

'What's his name?' I ask.

She looks at the picture. Her smile takes a wide stance. 'My husband's name is Casey. From our honeymoon in Barcelona.'

I don't correct her, but I was asking about the dog.

She regards me intensely, folding her hands over her desk. 'Why are you here, Joanne?'

'Because I cut myself.'

She shakes her head. 'I don't mean that literally. I can see that you've cut your wrists.'

I want to correct her; it is my forearm, not my wrist. More specifically, the basilic vein that drains the blood to my upper body. A doctor should be accurate if nothing else. But this isn't the response she wants.

My mother was Baker Acted thirteen times before her death. I know what people like her want to hear from me. 'I've been feeling very sad, but it's a one-off incident. I don't normally have thoughts of hurting myself.'

It's an obvious lie, but she grins. I've said the correct thing.

She consults my chart, which is just a file folder with my last name spelled wrong in the upper right-hand corner. 'You're being held for seventy-two hours, as per Florida law. But you seem stable. I don't see it being any longer than that.'

I look at my arm, the gash under wraps. A schematic bleed. That's what it would have been. My blood cells are lost in a basin of red, drowning in exposure to open air. She can't see that I wanted to leave this world like my mother did.

But.

I can't tell her that.

'It's Andersen, with an E.'

'I beg your pardon?'

'You've spelled my name wrong in your file.'

She assures me, 'I will take care of that.'

I doubt her, and severely.

A different orderly leads me from her office, escorting me to my room. I am in a hospital gown and the same makeup stains from last night. Everyone can see my behind *again*, and the mascara streaks on my cheeks are crunchy and stale. My legs are unshaven, and there's a strand of black hair growing on the cleft of my chin. My arms are wrapped up, but scarlet lines peek from under the gauzy surface.

The walls seem to laugh with their mocking white paint. The elevator is stuffy and smells like pee. A nurses' station greets me, but the nurses themselves are more placeholders than medical staff. Their chubby arms are packed into bright-coloured scrubs, and their lips part like filleted salmon.

We interrupt their stream of gossip. They all look annoyed at the orderly, then at me. The lead salmon rolls her eyes and tells us, 'Room 283, bed two.'

I share a room with two other women and a smattering of half-dead roaches. Our mattresses are on the floor. Nobody knows why. The girl with the mermaid doll isn't here.

I do not know why I expected to see her at all.

~

On top of the daily sessions, thrice a week is group therapy with Dr Maxine. Monday, Tuesday, Friday, we are crammed into a room with blue plastic chairs set in an oblong circle. This time I see the mermaid girl, still forlorn and clutching her doll with despair. Her fingers work like nooses, wearing down the skin around her neck.

We go around and introduce ourselves.

Several men are alcoholics. A few women have been abused. Most everyone is here because they have hurt themselves in one way or another. The mermaid girl speaks. Her voice is a tense purr. 'I'm Miranda.'

Dr Maxine asks, 'How are you feeling?'

She nibbles the tip of her thumb and shrugs.

'Now, now. That's not an answer.'

I want to fight the doctor. Though I don't know this girl, something about her makes me afraid for her and inclined to protect.

'Tired,' Miranda says. 'My roommate was screaming all night.'

The doctor tells her that's normal.

Miranda sighs. 'Screaming scares me a lot.'

Dr Maxine ignores her pain. She says, 'Miranda, you have the doll again. What did we talk about last time, dear?'

I want to punch her in the face, once for Miranda, once for the doll.

A woman with white hair speaks up. 'Damn doll's so ugly, I'll take it myself. Shit.'

Miranda puts her head down and doesn't speak again for the rest of the hour. I don't

speak either. There's nothing to say. I made a mistake. I don't belong here.

And I need to find a way to get out.

At the end of group therapy, I'm given a journal to 'write all my deepest thoughts and interpersonal feelings.' It is cheap and black and dented at the corner.

'I only use mine for drawing.'

I jump out of my skin, but when I turn, it's just Miranda. Her head is down, and she's still biting at her thumb.

'I like your doll,' I tell her.

This makes her grin, a little bit. 'I really like mermaids.'

'Mermaids are cool.'

Her chin shoots up. 'Do you want to see my room?'

~

Miranda's corner of the room is covered in mermaids of all kinds. Mermaids clipped from magazines, with CGI fins and bright, animated eyes. Cardboard pictures taped or glued to the decade-old paint. Sloppily drawn mermaids in felt-tip marker and crayon. Mermaids in a rainbow. Mermaids drowning in haphazard water with white space in between. All on pages ripped from the therapy-issued composition books.

It's comforting, the way she has made this space her own.

We are on the same floor, a few rooms apart. The nurses were so wrapped up in their conversations, they didn't notice her sneak me by and into her makeshift grotto. While I look at her drawings, she curls up on her bed, flanked by a collection of identical plush mermaid dolls.

'My mother never let me have dolls,' she tells me. 'My parents are divorced. Whenever I visited my father, he would buy me a Little Mermaid doll because it's my favourite movie. Once I got back home, she made me put it in a bin up in the attic.' A shadow crossed her face. 'I never understood why.'

'You're grown now,' I say. 'You can have all the mermaids you want.'

'Only so many in here,' she says. 'And no porcelain, that's contraband.'

'When you get out, you can get whatever you want.'

Her lips tip into a smile, but it's a laborious beam. 'It's requiring patience, which I'm not the best at, I'm afraid.'

'I understand that. I'm the least patient person ever.'

'We have a few things in common.'

My eyes float from one mermaid to the next. Eventually, I ask, 'How long have you been here?'

She tells me, 'Six months.'

'Yikes.'

Her teeth probe a cuticle. 'I have a lot of problems, comorbidities galore. Intrusive thoughts, bad nightmares. I'm afraid of... everything.'

We stay silent for a while. Her screaming roommate is asleep; the only noise is the subtle hum of the humid air conditioning.

Miranda touches my arm. I didn't hear her come up behind me. 'What did you do, seriously? I promise I won't tell.'

I pull myself away, wanting to tell her nothing is wrong. Ironic, considering we are in a literal psychiatric unit. When I turn to face her, my mouth surprises me by admitting, 'I went for a big swim and got a big cut.'

~

There is one chapel for people of all faiths, but the man at the lectern is Catholic. I reach for the Star of David necklace I've forgotten isn't there.

We're allowed out to eat, smoke and worship God. I don't smoke. The food is rancid. But I could always use a rabbi. There isn't one here, though, just a priest with a beer gut and alcohol-scented sweat. Some girls talk to him, but I sit in the very back with my notebook and green crayon. No pens or pencils, and the felt tip markers had already been claimed.

I sit in the chapel until lights out.

I don't write.

I don't draw.

I just think.

About how I was found face down in a lake by an old woman and her decrepit, snotty dog. She called the police – as women like her do. I was half-conscious after attempting to slice open my veins. I had jumped in the water after. Saw that in a movie once. There was no bathtub, but Lake Baldwin would do in a pinch.

So I assumed.

It wasn't true.

The cop arrived shortly thereafter, thinking me drunk and disorderly.

'What are you doing, ma'am?' he barked at the darkness.

I turned over and told him, 'Going for a swim. Don't mind me.'

It was then he saw the cut, the purple lids beneath my eyes, and the ghostly sheen of my skin and called for backup. And an ambulance.

Stat.

It feels like a decade ago, and not a single day. The wounds were superficial. Syncope had made me faint. I wish the cop had left me. I wish he'd let me sink.

I don't belong here.

I will get out, one way or the other.

~

The next day in group therapy, we talk about our upbringings. Miranda picks at the white lines on her arms while another woman speaks of her mother becoming violent, hitting her with whatever objects she could get her hands on.

'Do you remember those days?' the man next to me says.

I cannot nod. My mother wasn't like that.

Dr Maxine turns to Miranda, prods her into speech. 'I know you have something to contribute to this conversation, right hon?'

The whites of Miranda's eyes glow like pearls. She cries, and they turn green, then blue, purple, and even red. They settle on a shade of pink as she collects herself. 'I remember being regularly beaten with wooden boards. Really, anything. Having my mouth scrubbed out for little things.'

She is clearly done talking, but Dr Maxine presses her to go on. When she shakes her head, the doctor says that she must. 'I won't let you sit and be quiet. We talked about this.'

Miranda wraps her hand around her throat, pressing a finger into her jugular notch. 'Before the divorce, my parents fought a lot. The holidays were always a nightmare. Screaming and hollering, Thanksgiving turkeys thrown out the door, and I would get smacked because I dared to ask questions.'

I want to reach across the circle, take Miranda in my arms and protect her.

She reminds me so much of…

No.

Miranda sinks into herself, thoroughly humiliated and emotionally spent. Satisfied with the 'sharing,' Dr Maxine turns to me. 'What about you, Joanne?'

'What about me?'

'Do you have anything to say about this?'

I shake my head; that is not why I'm here. My life was good.

'Must not have been too good,' a guy with a Betty Boop tattoo says. 'Otherwise, you wouldn't be here.'

My composure slips to the floor. 'Things happen. My mother did her best.'

Someone across the room scoffs. Miranda wipes her eyes.

'I knew your mother,' the white-haired woman says. 'Was in here a lot. Always carrying one of those Cabbage Patch dolls and crying her eyes out. I remember Gwen. Yes, ma'am, I do. Seems like every fifteen days she'd be back in here again.'

I breathe once, twice.

Will this woman knock it off?

She continues, 'Didn't she kill herself or something?'

The doctor doesn't stop this. In fact, she encourages her to share.

'Heard she did it in the Walmart bathroom, shit on the walls and everything. Shot herself in the middle of her shift. Some poor kid walked in and saw it, that's what I heard. Lordy, I never heard of such a mess!'

I want to tell her off. This woman doesn't know shit. Sure, she wore a tinfoil hat on her head. This was a habit; she was scared of the cornflower sky somehow absorbing her human soul. And the pills were an accident. She sometimes lost control in a world where she felt too crazy to belong.

I couldn't help her.

Now, I can't even help myself.

The chaos of the room fades when I find Miranda's eyes. I stare long enough for her to turn away.

'You're too young to be here,' the woman continues. 'Told your mama that too, both of you were too young to have all these kinds of problems.'

'I do not have problems,' I said. 'I had one suicide attempt.'

'That's all it takes,' the woman reminds me. 'Before you get lost in this shit system.'

I have no intention of staying in this system. Once is an instance, and I was overwhelmed with my grief, nothing more.

'What were you doing the day you tried to commit?' a man with scars around his thumbs asks me. He tried to cut them off once, he was 'so fucking high.'

I was visiting my mother's grave. It was the one-year anniversary of her passing. I'm not ready to share this. Instead, I just shrug and say, 'Dunno. Nothing special.'

Dr Maxine reminds me, 'That's not a good enough answer! Remember, we speak in complete sentences and share what we really feel.'

I sit up straight. 'Dr Maxine, do you really want to know how I feel?' Before I know it, I'm on my feet, voice leaving me in rage, like the witch herself had poured a potion down my throat. 'I think this is bullshit! Yeah, I tried to kill myself! So what? Like that makes me any more special than the rest of you?' I turn to the white-haired woman, who shrinks in her withered skin. 'It wasn't the bathroom, it was the parking lot. My mother was dead in the back seat, crumpled like an old rag doll. She had a stressful life. You can't blame her for wanting out. I don't blame her at all. No! I blame myself.'

Everyone in this room has led a worse life than I, yet they stare at me with pity and remorse.

Dr Maxine attempts to regain control. 'How do you feel now, Joanne?'

I don't answer her. Though I'm not allowed to leave, I stalk out the door, tears falling like raindrops from a weeping willow.

~

I stay in my room until after night-time when I can't wait for the restroom anymore. Miranda is there at the sink, furiously washing her hands.

'I've been here for an hour,' she says, wiping her nose on her wrist. I know she's been crying, but she wants to pretend otherwise, so I play along.

'I hate this,' she says. 'The cafeteria served crab cakes for lunch. I'm allergic to crab. They said my food was safe, but I couldn't touch it or the tabletop. At least, I really tried not to. But I can't be too sure. Anaphylaxis is no fun. I've never been in anaphylactic shock, but what I've read makes it sound like no fun, you know?'

She brings the faucet to a halt before turning it back on. 'I'm not sure if I'm allergic to crab, actually. My stomach hurts when I eat it. What if I am?' A hunk of un-lathered soap sits in her rosy palm. 'My mom hates me for this, among other things, but she never understood that I can't stop.'

She cuts the water with the tip of her hand, and all I can think is, *How on earth can anyone hate you?* I've known her for two days, and I would marry her tomorrow.

'I'm sorry,' Miranda says. 'Things have always been so hard, and it's worse because I feel nobody understands.'

I want to make her feel better. 'When I was a kid, we were so poor, me and my mom ate garbage. It's not so bad if you find food that hasn't been opened. People throw away good things sometimes.'

She stands still at the sink, watching me from the mirror.

'Or, for a time, she was a waitress, and sometimes she'd make no money. I'd sneak back into the kitchen and eat chicken fat from the fryer. It gave me diarrhoea.'

A small fit of giggles fights its way up from the anxious lump in her gut.

'I love you,' I tell her.

She shakes her head. 'You've known me for two days.'

'Miranda—'

She puts a sudsy finger to my mouth and says, 'Jo, don't do this.' As she walks away, the finger glides across my lips. I taste where she touched, and the soap slides underneath my teeth. I wonder if this is what it's like to have your mouth washed with soap. I walk to the sink, fill my hands with water and rinse the taste of 'I love you' from my tongue.

~

Dr Maxine does not have a clear diagnosis, so she makes me an alphabet soup: MDD. GAD. BPD. PTSD. A little IED for flavour.

'I don't think you're a danger to yourself or anyone else, so when the seventy-two hours are up, I'll recommend your release with outpatient care. Anger management as well, grief counselling for your loss, and some medications to ease your symptoms.

I tell her, 'Okay,' shut my ass up, and take my pills exactly as prescribed.

None of this will help.

It never helped my mother.

After our visit, I am back on my bed with the journal on my lap. I am writing mean thoughts in this little diary.

I HATE DOCTOR MAXINE
I LOVE MIRANDA
I MISS MOTHER
I MISS MYSELF
MOTHER FUCKING FUCK
FUCK

I do this on repeat until dinner time. At which point, I find Miranda. Her plate is full of vegetables that she will not attempt to eat. She was prescribed a hefty dose of Seroquel right before I came, and it's finally kicking in.

She feels like shit.

'Have you ever taken Seroquel?' she asks.

'Probably, at some point.'

She stares at me, miserable.

'Oh, you mean prescription? No, all my drugs were recreational.'

'That sounds dangerous.'

'Eh,' I tell her. 'I have a high tolerance for pills and pain.'

Miranda brings her knees to her chest, cradling the mermaid doll between her pinched thighs. Her toes tap the air like she's swimming. For once, she's not biting her nails.

'Have you hurt yourself before?' she asks.

I say yes.

It is the truth.

'Not necessarily intentionally, but I used to slam my head on walls when frustrated. Did it in the emergency room the other day, actually. It was nice to black out for a minute or two. Though I always wish it was longer.'

Miranda is so engrossed in the conversation, she doesn't notice the white-haired woman come up from behind. In an instant, the precious doll has been snatched from her timid hands.

'Hey!' she cries, letting her tray crash onto the floor. Her lettuce scatters like seaweed and gets squashed beneath her feet. The woman doesn't relent, holding the mermaid above her head. Miranda screams, ragged noises.

In an instant, I'm up from the table. I punch the lady.

Once.

Twice.

Before she hits the ground, she tosses the doll into the rafters. The orderlies are beside us now, separating us by force. Miranda is limp, staring at the dusty attic that now holds her doll.

No one will take it down.

That much, I know.

I see in her eyes as a flashback encloses her like flames licking at a burning house. She deflates as she is dragged off on her close-knit heels.

~

Later that night, I find Miranda face down in the bathroom, her rear cheeks sticking up like deoxygenated bubbles. A blood stain blooms like a rose on the wall, and tile sinks like violet sand beneath her corpse.

I should call an orderly.

A nurse.

Dr Maxine.

Anyone.

Instead, I kneel at her side. There is a faint pulse under the tide of her wrist.

'You aren't dead,' I say. 'You are swimming with the mermaids.'

It hurts to see this twice. I think of my deceased mother, finding her in the car, waiting to call for help, deciding, in the end, what's the point? There is no helping someone who feels trapped like the little mermaid under the sea. I won't take that from her. It's clear she's lost enough.

The wind shifts around us, her soul rising from her flesh like perfume.

Now, she is a daughter of the air.

ANASTASIA JILL

Anastasia Jill (she/they) is a queer writer living in Central Florida. She has been nominated for *Best American Short Stories, The Pushcart Prize*, and several other honors. Her work has been featured or is upcoming with *Poets.org, Sundog Lit, Pithead Chapel, Contemporary Verse 2, OxMag, Broken Pencil*, and more.

BELOW THE HORIZON
Anita Goveas

THE lights always flickered before they went out.
They flickered through Leena, tickled her retinas,
fluttered in her chest, but she had to watch them from
under lowered eyelashes. Her mother would make
her lie down in the quiet room if she noticed. She
counted the squares on the screen window until the
temptation went, the numbers lining up in her head.

Father was late; he'd have slowed down in the
frantic Mumbai traffic like a tortoise in a sea of
scuttling yellow beetles. Rickshaws navigated by
sound anyway. The honking didn't stop for anything,
let alone the blackouts, but Father liked to be sure of
his way forward.

A rhythmic jingling, pattering sound meant
Mother was in the kitchen, chopping steadily, up to
her wrists in gooey bindi and fragrant onions, her
bangles dancing. The night before Aunty Valerie
visited always meant a flurry of cooking, of dishes
that only appeared on the table when she was there.
Four or five hours of cooking to prepare for a visit
that usually lasted half that. Aunty never stayed over
like their other relatives. Leena wanted to ask why
she always left so soon, to ask what about their
family urged her to brevity but didn't because her
mother never did. Maybe it was another thing the
adults had decided she didn't need to know.

The pattering stopped. Mother would be staring at
her reflection in the gleaming surface of a ladle or
pan. Any shiny surface distracted her; she would
contemplate the curve of her threaded eyebrows or

her powdered cheek, ignoring any distortions from the vessel. Leena always had more patience with this need than her father, but sometimes she wished her mother would notice her that way, would notice what she was really like. There were no photos of either Mother or Leena in the house, only Aunty Valerie's sketches of family portraits, so perhaps Mother needed these periodic reminders of her own existence. Leena liked to watch her shadow stretch and recede in whatever light filtered through the apartment windows. That seemed the best way she imprinted on the world.

Leena closed her eyes and walked over to their ancient teak sideboard, some great-aunt's idea of a legacy, and felt for the cutlery. The apartment wasn't pitch black; the sun hadn't completely set, and the sky was slate grey, turning to charcoal, but Leena had grown up in the near-dark, and it still comforted her. The preparation for Aunty Valerie evenings made her stomach bubble and her palms itch at the same time. She laid out the silver forks with their squared-off ends on their small mahogany table. So much destruction in that room, of precious trees that would never grow back. If Leena ever mentioned it, Father's mouth would purse up, Aunty Valerie would pat her hand, and Mother... Mother would stare into the blade of a polished knife as if it would save her. Leena didn't really mind. Mother hadn't asked to have a daughter with the same wide, smooth forehead and same unfortunate affliction but who grew spider plants in every nook in the house. Leena kept her hair long and tightly plaited the way her mother asked her to, the way her father expected, but she couldn't tame her yearning to dip her hands into soil. She found her neatness in the way numbers lined up in her head, in the beauty of the Fibonacci sequence uncurling a leaf.

Her foot hit the sideboard when she went back for the matching knives, her knee slotting into the dent she'd made flailing about during her first fit. She didn't remember much about it, but she'd pieced together fragments from the comments her father made whenever the lights went out. She'd been about five years old, the fluorescent tube light in their old kitchen had started blinking, she'd been holding a metal Air India toy plane. Father had walked into the room to find Leena lying on the floor, shaking, her mother lying beside her with her eyes closed. He'd immediately diagnosed a folie a deux. After checking temperatures and pulses, he'd prescribed bed rest for Leena in the dark and the quiet. Mother had mostly grown out of her epilepsy triggers by then, but she never sat in front of a camera, and she often held one slim hand in front of her left eye whenever she crossed a threshold.

Mother had held both hands in front of her face the day they'd moved into this first-floor apartment in Malad. It had three bedrooms, a wide front room, a tiny kitchen and a tinier washroom. And no garden. They hadn't brought much of their old furniture: the sideboard, the aluminium pots, the old black-and-white TV that only Father watched but Leena was allowed to listen to if she sat with her back to it and stayed quiet. They'd watched the news together that way two days ago when VP Singh resigned because he'd lost the government's confidence. Mother had been lying down in the quiet room, Aunty Valerie had phoned, and Father had turned up the sound on the TV until he was alone in the front room (before Leena had crept back in because she didn't know where else to go). The quiet room had only become her space after she returned from hospital; there was no reason why Mother shouldn't be in there. Except it was the only place Leena kept her logic problems and film soundtracks, the things she collected now after all her toy planes had disappeared in the move. It was where she hid the pages of equations she created, the ones she pored over in all their beauty, that she couldn't share with anyone.

Pockets of air shimmied through the window. The weather was cool for September, but Leena missed the fresh breeze that had always danced around their old flat near Juhu Beach. The mosquitos were already buzzing against the screen; she'd have to light the coil. She felt for the tape player, pressed the centre button and swayed to 'Aate Jaate Hanste Gaate,' feeling the rhythm through the thin soles of her worn plastic chappals.

'Beta,' her mother's low, sweet voice cut through the music, 'did you light the candles?'

Leena felt her way back to the sideboard and stretched her fingers to the second drawer down, the fancy drawer with the napkins and candles they saved for best. Her fingers felt the rough slide of paper, the flow of linen but nothing smooth and solid. One of her weekly chores was to check the torches and replenish the candles, but she'd spent the afternoon pinching the dead leaves off her spider plants. The spindly tendrils took too much energy away, stopped new growth.

She couldn't slip out to the store; Father could be back any minute. The spider plants already made him shake his head and pull at his moustache. She might have some candle ends in the quiet room; she liked to save items that her parents would throw away. Broken shoelaces, pottery shards, old cassettes. Maybe someday she would fix them all.

She kept her secrets behind the divan, in a space she'd forged between the cushions and the wall. Leena squeezed her eyelids tightly together and clung to the front room wall until it curved into the hallway, then groped for the left-hand door, the one with the jet-black beaded curtain. No beautiful strings of crystals in this apartment; they caught stray shafts of light too easily. The rounded beads were cool and polished against her fingers and always jangled a little; she could find this room by following their sound. And it smelt different. Her parents' room smelt of her father's paan and her mother's jasmine perfume, hers of earthy plant pots. This one smelt like a library, papery and safe, because of the books and newspapers that always seemed to find their way in there.

Sometimes, when the light had danced too hard, and she was lying down with her eyes closed while the sparks danced through her brain, her mother would read to her. Always from the same book of fairy tales, and always the same ones. The Fisherman and the Jinn. The Wolf and the Fox. The Queen of the Serpents. Leena's favourite was a tale of a woman who was willingly locked in a tower to protect her daughter, who was a great princess. Because of her sacrifice, she was granted one wish. Leena always fell asleep before the ending, but she often dreamed the princess rode to the rescue and the two lived happily ever after.

She settled down on the soft, cushioned seat and fumbled in the gap behind. Leena brushed against the sleek cover of an old magazine until she found the edges of her cardboard treasure box, an old tissue box she'd also rescued. But when she pulled it out, it was cardboard and flat, some type of document folder. She didn't remember hiding this. Inside, the first piece of paper was from St Joseph High School, the good behaviour certificate she'd got in Second Standard, three days before she never went back. The next was the first story she'd written, when she was six years old, about a tiger who ate carrots and had very bright eyes. A times-tables test covered with ticks. An old spelling test, covered in red pen. Underneath, the papers were covered in letters and equations and had a different name, Maria Rebello, and a different school, Sophia College for Women.

Her worst fit had been the one that ended up in flashing lights and a broken ankle. She'd been in the garden of their Juhu flat, sitting on a swing, trying to time the crickets jumping under their tallest palm tree. Father was still at the Nanavati Hospital, and Mother was making green chicken curry while their maid Aarthi cleaned the bathroom. The sun was sinking below the horizon, and the light had shifted, a stray wisp of cloud or a shadow from the neighbouring garden, and she'd stood up on the swing to watch the patterns. Then the whole world shifted, and she had woken up in a very white room with the blinds pulled down, attached to a covered box that beeped, with her ankle feeling dull and sore. She ate yoghurts and boiled eggs, swallowed a tablet that made her hands shake and measured time by the number of meals. Her mother and Aunty Valerie had brought her pista kulfi and masala chai, which they fed to her from a tiny plastic spoon, and a cassette player and tapes. She hadn't seen her father until the night he brought her home in a taxi with her foot in a box, and she'd slept until the next afternoon. Leena never saw the tablets the hospital gave her again.

She never went back into the garden either. Her ankle had healed slowly, and her father told her, in his voice like stainless steel, that she was safer at home until it mended properly. Bones were tricky, sensitive things, like brains. She'd believed him, then. Playing cricket with her school friends faded away, so did school. She could do her homework lying on the settees in the front room, in front of the shrouded television; later, she finished assignments in the quiet room. There didn't seem to be any other children in the whole new whitewashed apartment building, her parents seemingly having stumbled on a retirement colony, a place where the occupants decorated their living spaces with bright wall hangings and overstuffed bookcases but stored bags of rice on their balconies. Still, she somehow pieced together enough information to pass her Secondary School certificate, although no one talked about how she would use it. Leena found out later Aunty Valerie had insisted.

Aunty Valerie had brought the first spider plants, brought Leena the soundtrack to 'Maine Pyar Kiya,' a film she could imagine from the glossy stills in the newspaper and the fizzing lyrics. Aunty Valerie visits made Leena's stomach bubble and her palms itch at the same time. Aunty Valerie dinners consisted of foods she'd noticed weren't on the table at any other time: dry-fried bindi, fish fry, cauliflower pilau. The food always tasted more savoury, richer somehow. Father didn't eat fish, liked plain vegetables or rotis, but he never complained. For the first time, Leena wondered why.

Mother was studying her mangolsutra when Leena stormed into the kitchen, a pot of coconut-laced kingfish curry bubbling on the hob, sweet and sour. She didn't look up, but Leena didn't need her to this time.

'You went to college' – Leena waved the page of equations – 'you studied, and you never told me. Why wouldn't you tell me?'

Mother reached over to stir the pot, then turned off the heat. The spices needed time to infuse.

'I felt my place was in the home,' she said softly, sweetly, as she did everything. Only her need to examine her features went against her gentle presence. 'There were too many risks in the way the world might treat me, your father explained. I believed him, then.'

Leena pointed to the neat row of letters at the bottom of the page, the ones she'd smudged when she rescued it from its hiding place.

'But you don't believe him now? Is that why you're still studying? Does he know?'

Mother turned her back, her bangles jingling as she chopped garlic into paper-thin slivers.

'Leena, some things don't need to be told.'

Leena saw her own reflection in the pot of fish curry, her thick curly hair, her unruly eyebrows. Her gritted teeth in her set mouth.

'But if you knew I wanted to go to college, why wouldn't you tell me this?'

The pile of garlic grew, pale and fragrant. The knife thudded against the wooden chopping board like tiny heartbeats.

'It's different for you, you've never even been to school. I can manage if I narrow my focus. Any shaft of light could strike you down,' Mother said, the knife flashing.

All those times in the quiet room, when her mother read her to sleep, when the gentleness was soothing. All those times when her mother thought she was weak.

'Is this why Aunty Valerie is allowed to visit, why you cook all this food Father won't eat?'

Mother chopped at the skin of a piece of ginger, slicing away until the heart emerged.

'If there was a story about a woman who had sacrificed her heart's desire' – Mother paused to extract a shred of ginger peel with a perfectly oval fingernail – 'why wouldn't she be granted one wish?'

Leena fled back into the quiet room, the air in the kitchen too thick with pungent smells. She passed her rows of spider plants, a mass of green like a silent army. Spider plants grew unstoppably if you didn't let them rot. They didn't need much water and hardly any light. They'd worked out a way to thrive without much care. She found some candle stubs in a chipped carved wooden cabinet and felt her way back into the front room to finish her task. In the flickers of candlelight, the shadow of her own body was too long and uncontained. Nothing in the room seemed to fit round it. Strands of the spider plants hanging in the nooks and crannies fluttered round her shadow head like a crown, like a shawl. They seemed to be the only things that suited her now. Her shadow stretched further, one thin arm escaping out the apartment window. Leena longed to follow it, but she knew what her mother and father would say. She heard the motorized putter of a rickshaw stopping outside.

It was an Aunty Valerie night tomorrow. Her Aunty, who always brought her precious fragments of the world. Who brought the spider plants and the music. Who she had never wanted to escape from. Who had made sure she had her school certificate, who had offered an escape that she hadn't noticed. But she noticed now.

ANITA GOVEAS

Anita Goveas is British-Asian, London-based, and fuelled by strong coffee and paneer jalfrezi. She was first published in the 2016 *London Short Story Prize* anthology, most recently by the *Cincinnati review*. She's on the editorial team at *Flashback Fiction*, and tweets erratically @coffeeandpaneer. Her debut flash collection, 'Families and other natural disasters', is available from *Reflex Press*, and links to her stories are at https://coffeeandpaneer.wordpress.com

THE SHINY PEOPLE
Heather Haigh

JOAN creaks out of the shower and wraps herself in a thick towel, clinging to a vestige of warmth. She shudders; another patch of rust on her forearm is growing. She recalls Brian's medieval gauntlet, damp after his re-enactment weekend, ruined by rust in the space of days. The floorboards creak as she clanks to her bedroom workbench. Cure-rust for her arm, wire-wool for the scratches criss-crossing her face, she finishes off with multi-purpose metal polish all over.

~

Rain-laden, pewter clouds hang in a nickel sky. Her feet hit the pavement with resounding thuds as she heads for the charity shop at the end of Towngate. The voices that rattle around in her head begin their morning ritual.

Volunteering isn't real work. Too old. Too stupid. Too weird.

Joan judders to a halt and thwacks her head on a peeling silver birch.

They only let you help because they couldn't find anyone better.

As her head meets the nearest lamp post, she curses at the thought of how long the damage will take to buff out.

How does Margaret, always ready to greet Joan with a smile, start her day? Joan's mind fills with an image of copper pans hanging by a blazing hearth,

Margaret kneading bread dough, surrounded by clouds of flour, the air thick with yeast and cinnamon. Margaret would have contemporary music playing in the background, and she'd know the words.

~

The kettle is already whistling when Joan clunks into *ReachOut*. Margaret proffers sticky flapjack, rich with the scent of ginger. Joan's crumpled custard cream wrapper sits in the bin.

'Your hair looks lovely.' Joan nibbles the flapjack. Wonders if the compliment was cringeworthy. Feels herself shrinking, hears the grating of metal as her skin shifts to accommodate the tiny woman within.

'Thanks. That'll be the sun.'

Joan nods. 'How was Majorca?' That's got to be safe, hasn't it?

'Great. We met up with our friends, the Ademars, again. If you ever fancy it, you could join me and Ann for the shopping. The boys prefer their golf.'

Joan smiles and sips the sweetened brew, wondering if she should work a little more lubricant into the corners of her mouth. She doesn't know the correct response.

'You going away this year?' Margaret wipes a sliver of oat from the corner of her mouth with a soft pink finger. Neat. Dainty. Nothing clumsy about Margaret.

'Maybe Scarborough... or perhaps I'll potter around the garden – it could do with the work....'

Joan satisfies herself with the lightest tap to her head, aware that the metallic ring is jarring. She blinks back images of her last holiday with Brian. She'd promised him she would visit Scarborough again and remember him. As though she'd ever forget the silly old fool.

~

When she noticed the others at breakfast – the loud woman with platinum hair and an armful of bejewelled bracelets, the silver-haired one with designer sunglasses and a string of pearls, the men with their mirror-glaze shoes, razor-edged pocket handkerchiefs and sharper conversation, Joan shrank into her chair.

But Brian sat straight, then leaned across and whispered, 'Just be yourself. We don't need gilt and glitter like the shiny people. All buff and no substance.'

And she tried. She tied her hair back in a neat ponytail, gave herself a spritz of *Lily* and strode out. With Brian by her side, she tried.

~

'I wonder who donated this; it must have been special to someone.' Margaret's voice yanks Joan back into the present. Margaret pulls out a sunshine-yellow duster and rubs soundly at the gold-plated trophy. 'I'll finish the box. You want to start on that sack?'

The sack at Joan's feet is one of the sturdy black ones with tie handles. She fumbles the knot open and pulls out a pink woman's coat. The collar is finished with neat white piping, and the buttons are tiny pearlescent beads. Joan runs the fine wool between her fingers. Probably worn at a wedding by the sort of woman who never wears the same outfit twice.

'That's a fine piece. We'll get a good few pounds for that.' Margaret's eyes sparkle; every penny made for the charity is a victory to relish.

Joan pulls out a coat hanger and finds it badly bent. She presses it against the ground, using her thumbs to coax it back into shape. When she slips the coat onto it, one shoulder droops. She sighs and rummages for a sturdier hanger. Even something that exquisite can't hide the twisted wire beneath.

~

The day passes quickly enough. A shuffle of bargain hunters, a trickle of time-passers, interludes spent with those who value fresh conversation over vintage clothing.

~

Margaret slips into the back for the keys to lock up. She returns with a small parcel in a Centro Commercial bag.

'You shouldn't have.' Joan means it.

'I wanted to. We couldn't do without you now. You deserve a treat. Open it when you get home.'

~

The familiar smell of *Lily of the Valley* hits Joan in a rush. She hasn't used it in years. Her hands tremble as she inhales the steam and watches the bubbles grow. She eases herself into the tub and tries to relax. Stupid. Fancy soaking in a bath. Soaking. What is she thinking? There'll be so much rust to deal with. No end of it. The rivulets down her cheeks will be the worst. Saltwater is so corrosive.

Fancy Margaret remembering. One chat, all that time ago. Joan had learned to keep the conversation light and right in the here and now. She was never making a show of herself in the shop again. But now...

She explores her face with soft fingertip pads, shocked to find damp, tender skin. A kaleidoscope of fragments glitters her bathtub. She pulls the plug, eases herself upright and watches a storm of rust flakes fall around her feet and swirl away. Joan prods at soft pink flesh. It feels vulnerable, naked, but oh so warm.

HEATHER HAIGH

Heather is an emerging disabled, working-class writer, from Yorkshire. She found the joy of writing late in life. Her words have been published by *Reflex Press, Anansi Archives, Mono* and others. She has been nominated for *Best of the Net*.
https://haigh19c.wixsite.com/heatherbooknook

YOU SEE FOOD, YOU EAT IT

Malik Berry

See, where he got me was when he told me he was a chef. My big fat ass almost fell in love right then and there.

I'd made a promise to myself that the next time I looked for some dick or ass, I'd find someone who could teach me something resourceful. Grindr doesn't do shit for anyone's confidence or standards, plus the interface is an eyesore. What got me to uninstall it instead of letting it sit and collect virtual dust was how one-track-minded it all was. People who said they were looking for friends but were mostly looking for someone to gossip to or to nod and agree with the bullshit they spat. I was far too smart and black to involve myself with pink twink drama. My days of answering 'sup' and low-angle dick pics were going away, at least until this new plan turned out not to work.

To put this plan into action, I went out in public, something I tend to avoid unless it's for essentials. I'd always wanted to go into Leon's on Park Avenue for a real reason outside of Pride Weekend afterparties, so what better reason than this?

For all the worse I expected going in there, either being the glistening elephant in the room or the walking eggplant with a body attached to it, it turned out to be pretty nice. Quiet as hell, compared to most clubs I've poked my head into or block parties I've busted it down at with enough liquid courage in me. Speaking of those, I only had one beer before a man approached me.

119

This was the chef.

He didn't lead with that, thank God, instead choosing to say I'd made the right choice coming to this bar instead of The Drinkery just around the corner. As if that would mean something to me.

He told me his name was Bruce, and I struggled not to make any jokes about *Die Hard*. The fact that he was a bald and stocky white man didn't help. To be real, though, he was way funny and more chill than that old Hollywood actor could be. I thought I was making a good friend, and not a whole lot would come out of the evening up until we started talking about work.

I don't have any shame about working as a teacher's assistant. The kids love me – as they should, look at me – and it keeps me active and working without doing the most. It just comes up short compared to what every other man I've been around does. Office assistants, IT techs, doctors, volunteer firefighters, theatre people. Once, I hooked up with a dude who helped develop a heartburn medicine. None of that shit really matters, but when you find yourself topping a big-shot doctor in his house that he actually owns, you start to realise how temporary it is, how set your place in the world has been.

When I told Bruce what I did, his response was a bit of the same I'm used to, a turn-up of his lips and a nod. Then he followed up with something a little out of pocket.

'You're better than me,' he said. 'Kids make me so mad I could shit.'

I laughed, of course, because I'd never heard anyone put it like that. Why would anyone say that anyway? How did they expect to be responded to?

'So what do *you* do?' I managed to get out, still recovering from that shock.

'I'm a chef.' He said it like it was no big deal.

'Like a *chef* chef or a cook?'

'Yeah, a *chef* chef. I work at the Oceanaire.'

The Oceanaire is a fancy seafood place in the Harbor East circle by the water with all the well-off people and financial types going in to chow down and do business. A far cry from getting a seafood boil from a place called Angie's after church or a party, so I knew I was out of my element with this dude.

My grandma always told me never to trust a cook who isn't fat. It's the one job where getting high on your own supply is a sign that you're the best. I humoured him and asked him to show me some of the stuff he made. He whipped out his phone, and he did. Of course, the dude was on TikTok, showing off dishes he made at the restaurant as well as on his own time. I was amazed by how anyone could cook for fun like it was recreational. Some days I get too lazy to put a pan down and wait for olive oil to start sizzling. Bruce here was throwing around lobster meat and chopping fresh veggies like it was nothing to him.

And that's what got me. He was nice but also skilled and didn't take himself seriously unless it came down to his cooking. Plus, I was selfish enough to think that if I spent the night, he'd whip up something high-class for me, so I could pretend I was living good.

That all went into the back of my mind once we committed to hooking up. We went back to his place, and of course, he lived in Bolton Hill, at that little circle with the fountain. He kept a window open for air, so I always heard the trickle of water from it whenever I was in his room. It was enough to make you wanna pee every other hour.

Being in his house had me flashing back to school, though. I went to one of those charter joints, the worst decision my parents ever made, honestly. Families of my classmates all had houses like this, acting like they'd moved on up or had already been there due to generations of being exceptional. Most of those kids went on to have their dreams broken trying to be Miss Juneteenth or the next Obama.

I was one of those exceptional brats, being primped and primed, trotted out like a damn show pony whenever they needed someone to be all well-spoken. It was when I first started acting out, putting less bass in my voice, and doing everything I thought a gay little black boy should do to keep everyone from wanting something out of him.

That shit can only take you so far because here I was, back in another place like those townhouses owned by those uppity Jack & Jill of America types. Had this been Harlem in the twenties, I'd have found my kind of people. Unfortunately, the wealthy black folk are nowhere near as artistically talented or amusing as anything the likes of Langston Hughes could fart out onto a page.

All this ran around in my head as if Bruce wasn't already sitting me down on his couch and pulling my shirt off. I came back to Earth when his hands ran all around my stomach, and I looked back into his eyes with a smile. I realised then that my situation was better than when I was growing up. I was sure of myself, comfortable enough to go back to a neighbourhood populated by attitudes I hated, even if only for a night with one nice, cute guy.

It was all so complicated, and I didn't have the mind to put it all together into some cohesive breakthrough. Believe it or not, when you're getting your dick sucked, your mind gets foggy, and nothing else matters but that warm feeling around you. Your hands start moving on their own either to rub yourself or to plant down on that smooth head bobbing up and down in your lap.

I returned the favour, of course, and we spent the time just lazing around, not ready to split ways and not energetic enough to go to the bedroom and do some proper fucking. Bruce wanted more, but I also wanted to see what it was like to watch him work his culinary magic. With some prodding and jokes, I managed to get it out of him. I could wait all week before.

Chefs don't take their work home with them, so I couldn't get to sample what sixty-dollar flash-seared scallops with butter tasted like. Instead, he just whipped up some steamed shrimp real quick and easy. Bruce even had the courtesy to break out the Cup Noodles with some actual garlic, green onions and Spam to mix it all with.

I was in disbelief. Not that I expected a chef to have some high-on-the-hog kind of cuisine sitting in his pantry all the time. Bruce isn't Gordon Ramsay; he's just a dude in Baltimore like me. My surprise came from how in-the-zone he was making something out of what tides you over before the food stamps come.

'If I can be real with you,' he said that night, 'I don't like the fancy shit I cook up either. It's good for the one quarter of the year you can afford it, but at the end of the day, I'll take something a little fast to get me through a day, even a shift.'

While he cooked, he had a bag of white fudge pretzels open to pop into his mouth now and then. I understood what he meant.

The food was great and had me thinking back again on what it feels like to be home and indulge in all that your family could scrape up. You take solace in the cheap shit when you're making good money. It serves as the perfect reminder that only the scenery and place have changed, not yourself. I even brought it up to Bruce, who was kind enough to stop staring at how I responded to his cooking to tell me he grew up in some town in Maine. Why he'd wanted to go further down south to here, he never answered straight on, but he seemed too confident for the reason to be escaping a conservative town. I just chalked it up to Maine being expensive as hell as I wiped the cocktail sauce from the corner of his mouth.

Since we were putting the kibosh on pounding each other, cuddling was the next best thing. Stomachs full and satisfied, breath no longer smelling of our musty skin and seed spilled between each other's lips, it was the kind of interaction only expected from a married couple. No one would dare think of gays being this lovely after a hook-up. We're all supposed to disappear like thieves in the night, trotting back to our public bathrooms and community theatre rehearsals as if nothing happened so we can prowl around and do it all over again, but this time with an assembly line of hairy-chested men with chests bigger than a supermodel.

As fun as all that sounds, when you're working and living simple enough, those brief moments are far more worthwhile than the constant jumping from one cock to the next, one hole to the next, one shot after the other to loosen you up for the overconfident sixty-year-old who keeps calling you different names for chocolate.

We did get each other's number afterwards and have fucked for real since then. Hard to say if we really got 'serious' after that, but Bruce is a sweetheart who I always hit up, always hang out with, always cradle in my arms after particularly intense nights at the Oceanaire. It's like an emotional support hook-up, something I doubt we even knew we wanted or needed, but damn if I'm backing out of it now.

It *is* love, don't get it twisted. Just the kind of love from people who need a shoulder to lean on and someone to take their most real side seriously, no need for a performance to back it all up. Since then, I've taken him to get that seafood boil at Angie's that I raved over. He could never finish it all, but it was always a blessing to come to his place and see the bag get less packed full of shrimp, sausage, corn and all the rest. I imagine it felt the same when he peeked through the kitchen door at the Oceanaire to see me and my momma being waited on.

It goes to show that a man who can cook is bad for your nerves but good for your heart.

MALIK BERRY

Malik Berry is a black nonbinary writer, film historian, and community organiser based in Baltimore, Maryland. This is their first story in physical print, having published fiction through digital publications like *The Junction* and *Pickle Fork*, and film criticism in *Film Inquiry*. Their plays 'To Love an Ass' and 'It Starts With a Spark' have been staged by *Rapid Lemon Productions* as part of their *Variations Project* in 2022 and in 2023. Malik is currently at work organizing a short story collection. You can connect with Malik on Twitter @malikb_wav and Tumblr @malikxberry.

DEAR NAME
Kyungseo Min

SEARCHING for an adventurous human female.

The ad asked no questions. It wasn't even a call to action. Yet, it emboldened her like a clean sheet of paper. Unblemished possibility.

She whispered, 'Yes,' and called the number right there in the near-empty corridor of that strip mall, where the faint smell of urine crept from the bathroom and a Top 40 song blasted from cheap speakers. A sterile voice guided her through the options. One, for service in English. Eight, for Project Neander. Four, for intake. She said her phone number, and the voice repeated it back to her in perfectly enunciated syllables. One, to confirm.

Ping.

She received the text message with the link to make an appointment. The website was simple and professional. Completely devoid of adventure.

What if the ad had asked if she was a human female ready for an adventure instead? But to be adventurous required no adventure.

A few weeks after responding to the ad, she received an invitation for evaluation.

Inside a cold room, far removed from the chill of spring, she filled out a questionnaire, sworn to an honesty only possible in paperwork.

What is your ethnicity?

The first two boxes were Caucasian and Black. Underneath was a grey arrow with a faint *Other* underneath. She clicked it, and it vomited out a list.

When she tried to click on multiple options, it wouldn't let her.

She kept trying, watching the other box uncheck itself each time. Each click tapped into an urge. An urge to jump off and impale herself on a corner. To let her blood fill in the square that contained everything and absolutely nothing. Red blood, not black or white or brown or yellow. Red.

She skipped the question and proceeded with the rest of the questionnaire. But when she tried to submit, she was faced with an aggravatingly respectful error message.

Please fill in the required fields.

The receptionist blinked at her. 'What's the problem?'

'Sorry, I…' An inhale. 'It won't let me choose more than one option for ethnicity.'

Option. As if she had a say. As if the world had asked for her preference.

The young woman blinked again, wiping the annoyance from her eyes and replacing it with a film of bland courtesy.

'Just choose other, then other again at the very bottom of the list. And fill out the text field with your… you know.'

An adventurous human female started at the bottom. It wasn't surprising. But the surprising unsurprisingness of it all poked and prodded at her.

When she submitted the form, she was given a number and told to wait until she was called. The tracker on the Now Serving monitor went up slowly. But the waiting room was empty. Who did those numbers beckon?

'Number eighty-eight. Eighty-eight. Please proceed to room B.'

It was her number. She stared at her empty hands and felt her toes inside her boots curl up. The dare of unblemished possibility suddenly turned into a threat, closing in around her throat. Her tongue felt too big for her mouth. It flopped, wanting to say something. Anything. She wasn't sure what. Yes? No? Maybe next time?

'Eighty-eight.' It was the receptionist. She looked up, and the woman pointed with her pen towards the hallway. Like a mindless sheep, she followed.

Maybe her tongue wanted to bleat. Bad, bad, bad idea.

It was surprisingly routine. They took her blood pressure, a blood sample, and a cheek swab for her DNA. They took her weight and measured her hips. She signed a medical record release form, so they could access every ache and pain she'd ever bothered to see a doctor about. She gave up these parts of herself willingly, almost enthusiastically. Something had changed. There was nothing she wanted more now because she realized that this was a test. She could be rejected for not being adventurous enough, not being female enough, not being human enough.

There was one more form: a form of consent. In the case they deemed her the most suitable, she would allow whatever they wanted to do to her body. It should've felt like a slave contract. Instead, she felt free. The entirety of her body would be their problem.

Smiling, she signed it and clicked submit.

When she received the e-mail notifying her that she had been chosen, it was too late to change her mind. She was enough. At least for their purposes. Whatever that meant.

And adventurous meant being bound to a hospital bed with countless machines hooked up to her for nine months. Beeping, hissing, humming. Counting and measuring what it meant to be alive. But being alive required no life.

The technician shook the bottle one, two, three times, then squirted the cold gel on her lower stomach. She didn't even flinch anymore.

Someone turned off the lights. The ultrasound monitor cast a hazy glow on the safety goggles in the room with its swirling grey storms.

'Looks good,' he said, but not to her.

She'd seen this technician every day for almost a year, but they had never made eye contact. She disliked how he touched her as some specimen when she was an adventurous human female. Now, she couldn't even bear the smell of his ultrasound gel.

He announced, 'I'd say December 31st.' Again, not to her. The other doctors in the room nodded and noted it down.

'Happy New Year,' she whispered to the untouched darkness in the corner.

The lights came back on. Without a word to her, they left. The automatic doors closed behind them with a beep and a hiss.

But she wasn't alone. She hadn't been truly alone for forty weeks. Gestating inside her were all her complexities shrunk to complications, wrapped in a neat placenta. The swirling storms rose to her throat.

Huffing, she reached over with her swollen wrists and fingers and tugged the blackout curtains aside. The window revealed a snowstorm. And the snowflakes were as delicate and angry as she was.

She wrote on the windowpane: *Dear*.

Her hand dropped. The chill on her fingertip sharpened a lingering question into focus.

What would she name the child?

She stared at the salutation until the 'D' trickled down into a 'p,' the 'a' into a 'q,' the 'r' into a morbidly long 'n.' When was the last time she had sent a letter? She had stopped sending them because she hated addressing the envelope. The destination boldly centre stage, and in the corner, the sender's address. Always small and always unassuming. Because a destination could be anywhere. The origin, however, was always singular. And that felt oppressive, like an act of violence that wrapped the contents of her thoughts with a lie she was forced to tell in a world that accepted only a 'but' and never an 'and.'

And every time she was asked, '*But* where are you really from?' she felt it. The small and modest, bent and wrinkled corner of the sender's address. All the letters she never sent. The sight of them in the garbage bin hardened her gaze, which people mistook for courage when it was actually strength. Strength that allowed her to face the questions that poked her again and again with constant and relentless curiosity.

The letters were now frozen nonsense on the windowpane. She smiled without moving her lips, an exhausted and desperately unhappy smile. They were indescribable, just like her.

December 31st came and was about to end. The technician was wrong. But they corrected that with a prostaglandin tablet.

No amount of strength could've prepared her for the final act of violence. Her insides folding – crumpling – twisting – it focused time into a thin, cold edge – push – a damp satisfaction as she finally felt her emotional rebellion manifest into reality – push – her hands curled into fists, but who would she shatter? Push – the moat of fear in her womb boiled over – push – is it possible to push out an entire sun? Push – there was no name to scream out – push – so she screamed sounds – push – she screamed – push – towards – she screamed towards – push push push – the edge of dawn –

Push.

The sun came out. And all its heat left her.

She dared not open her eyes. This was her throwing the ad and the adventurousness, the nameless and the blame, everything in these past nine months into the darkness behind her eyelids. The sounds of the doctors, nurses, technicians, and the crying... they were all devoured too. The only thing she could stomach right now was darkness.

Click. Click, click.

She felt her bed being wheeled away. They faded, all the voices, the footsteps... and the crying. But her ears hung onto its echo. The wailing resonated right there between her breasts.

When she opened her eyes, she was back in her room. There was a fresh layer of snow outside her window. The perfect white outlined the emptiness behind her outstretched and deflated belly button. Each quiet yet immense breath was a reminder that her loneliness was finally made perfect.

She was finally alone.

Before, she used to hate being alone. After these last nine months, it was all she wanted. When she had started to visibly show, she realized that it was only in solitude that she felt... neutral. Unblemished. Neither too this nor too that. In the middle, she felt possible.

And now that she was finally alone, she longed for its presence. But how would she call for it if she never gave it a name?

'Happy New Year, everyone!' the TV blared in the hallway.

She stared at her frozen handwriting. They compelled her to say it out loud. As her breath found voice, she couldn't stop. 'Dear... dear... d-dear...'

Dear who?

'It's the future today, and what screams more of future than scientific advancement?'

It was the least she could do, to repeat a blank placeholder until it capitalized into a real name.

'Yesterday night, the world welcomed its first Neanderthal – a distant relative to us homo sapiens.'

It was the least she could do, to call out a name that would never respond back. Not even as an echo.

'Thanks to genetic sequencing and advancements in cloning technology, we are now able to study the history of mankind.'

It was the least she could do, to call out a spell of love and contempt for a world that had ignored her so deeply she could no longer endure it.

'For thousands of years, we were the only species of genus homo alive. Now, with this baby Neanderthal, we will be able to answer the question: what makes us humans unique? Why did we survive, but they couldn't?'

As if giving birth could kill the sharp, grey arrow of *Other* that was lodged deep inside her. As if expelling a checkbox from a hole could make her fit somehow. As if emptiness could be filled by digging a deeper emptiness. She had believed that by giving birth to an other more other than her, she could become alike and liked.

And yes, she was alike. She had the same capacity for violence and felt the same bitter joy for destruction. She had the temerity to be disappointed at her own failed dare: to gestate a neat and tidy envelope containing all her otherness to be sent anywhere else, as long as it was far, far away.

But all she was left with were the wrinkled folds of her skin. She tried to smooth them out. It was impossible.

'Here to explain is Dr Church, lead researcher on this ambitious experiment. Dr Church, what are the next steps now that we have this test subject?'

Test subject. She wanted to protest, but what could she say?

A smooth voice of authority chuckled, then described a long list of research questions. About humans, history, anthropology. Focusing on differences. It was always the differences. There was no mention of similarities. Nothing about adventure. And nothing about her, the origin of this 'fascinating subject matter.'

The baby's destination was clear. It would live its life prodded, examined, studied. She had no words of encouragement as someone familiar with that path.

The TV laughed at some joke she didn't bother to hear. It mocked her and her solitude.

And she had no words of encouragement as a mother because being a mother didn't always mean being maternal.

She heard its crying again as if it was begging her for a name. But she had nothing. Her adventurousness was at an end. It was but a standstill journey that had no destination and not even a clear origin.

'My dear…' she whispered as she wiped her sweaty palm across the cold window, erasing the unfinished letter. A clean pane.

KYUNGSEO MIN

Kyungseo Min is a writer for video games, plays, and short stories. Her plays have been presented in Canada and Europe and her short stories have been published in Canadian and American print and online magazines. She currently works as a Narrative Designer on Overwatch 2.

Twitter: @kminminpow

Website: www.kyungseomin.com

POWER TO THE PEOPLE
A.M. Gautam

'**PAPA** is home,' the doorbell declared dutifully, a minute before the clock struck six.

Mummy tucked a loose strand of hair behind her ear, checked her appearance in the black kitchen tiles, and made sure that the newspaper was on the drawing-room table as Papa preferred it to be. Then she put on a smile and opened the door.

Papa nodded at her, removed his shoes, and entered the house. 'The children?' he asked.

'There was a field trip scheduled to the Shakha today, I think, but they should be home anytime now,' Mummy called after him and wondered if he had heard her over the sound of water in the bathroom. She did not repeat herself, however, because he could resort to the old belt-and-shoe treatment when she talked too much and irritated him. The bruise she earned last week for putting too much salt in the curry was still fresh on her back.

Papa changed into his kurta-pyjama while she got his tea ready and settled on the sofa with the newspaper, *The Good Times of India*.

'Hello?' Papa called out in the kitchen's direction. 'Is the dinner ready? You didn't forget about the Poll, did you?'

'No, of course not. I hope the children are not late. Baaba-Ji said in last week's broadcast that it was very important for children to learn about democracy as soon as possible.'

Papa sighed. This one was okay, he thought to himself, all things considered. He had been forced to report his first wife to the Mohalla Vigilance Committee for being anti-national. Not that he hadn't tried his best to put up with her, but the foolish woman just couldn't adapt to the changing times. He'd returned early from the office one day to catch her reading a book and had no choice but to report the grave offence. Even the Swayamsevaks at the Mohalla Shakha were shocked when he went to them. Only five cases of women reading books had been reported since the war, one of them told him when they came to cart her off. The next day they took away her children too, for fears of Idea-Infection.

'Sooraj and Amit are home,' the doorbell declared, bringing Papa out of his memories. Mummy went to open the door, and he turned a page of his newspaper. It felt almost like paper, as a courtesy to the old days, though actually, it was a disposable fibre screen that talked to the reader in a low voice about anything he wanted to know, that it wanted to let him know.

Now, it told Papa about the new settlement being set up in the wastelands of Kashmir. The first building, a glorious temple of Lord Krishna, had been inaugurated by Baaba-Ji yesterday in the presence of Governors from all the remaining states and two hundred and fifty-one Brahmin priests. Just looking at the golden building with its magnificent blue idol made pride surge through Papa's heart. It had taken Baaba-Ji only forty-seven days to implement the Final Solution in Kashmir during the last days of the civil war.

I will tell the children that story tonight, Papa decided as the boys came to the living room. They touched his feet and sat down on the ground. Sooraj had turned ten – the voting age – two days ago, and Amit was six. There would have been a girl too, nine years old now, but Papa's position in the Ministry of Rehabilitation and Reintegration gave him the privilege of up to two abortions.

He looked up from the newspaper and reflected that, all things considered, he was proud of the boys sitting at his feet. They were disciplined and obedient. Sooraj was going to get a medal the next Democracy Day for reporting a classmate who had been lying about being a Brahmin to attend their school. An honour like that was a sure-shot assurance of acceptance into a good college.

A few minutes later, Mummy also came to the drawing room, bearing three plates of sabji-roti in two hands. She looked so frail – as if you could close your fist around her and press until she burst like a small chuski-mango, Papa thought and imagined squeezing her breasts while she moaned like a cat in heat. He crossed his legs one over the other so that the boys wouldn't see the bulge in his pyjama.

Mummy sat down on the floor with the children and tried her best not to look at Papa while he took the first bite and gave his verdict. He took his time to chew his food thirty-six times, as recommended by his yog-guru in the Shakha, and swallowed without remark.

'Is it time yet?' he asked the room.

Mummy glanced at the wall clock, nodded, and passed him a remote from the table. He pointed it at the wall opposite the couch and pressed the single red rubber button. Immediately, the wall came to life, and their senses were washed over by a sudden deluge of vibrant colours, flashing texts, and many voices talking loudly over each other.

All of them, even the kids, recognized the loudest voice well enough. The Voice of the Rashtra. They heard it countless times every day in everything from news bulletins and Public Safety Announcements to the online auctioning of the Undesirables' properties. To an extent, this Voice had become the voice of their conscience. It spoke to them soothingly when doubts entered their minds, admonished them at the first sign of resentment against the current state of things, and assured them, always, of the righteousness of their anger against the Undesirables.

The clock struck seven, and the man to whom the Voice belonged came into focus on the wall-TV as everything else faded out. As always, he was dressed immaculately, almost shimmering with confidence and a hint of well-kept secrets. Heavy black spectacles rested on his nose, giving him an intellectual look set firm by the neat, almost mechanical, middle parting of his hair. He seemed to flow like a wave on the wall-TV when he walked from one end of his studio to the other.

'Good evening, brothers and sisters,' said the Voice. 'I'm proud to welcome you once again to the cornerstone of our new democracy and the unique strength of our great Rashtra: The People's Poll.

Brought to you by Virgo Toothpaste, Bajrangi Cement and Steel, and of course, the invaluable blessings of Baaba-Ji.

'For our new viewers who have just turned ten, let me introduce you to the Poll, though no doubt you are already familiar with it. As you know, we had a Parliament once and courts where corrupt elitists pretended to be representatives of the common people. When the Undesirables dragged the nation into a war, their main complaint was that this Parliament and the courts were not democratic enough. The leaders were fascists, they said. That's how they explained their hatred of us.

'So, when Baaba-Ji won the war for us, he decided to give all the power directly to us. A true masterstroke, right?'

Here he paused to smile and sipped water from a glass.

'Citizens of the Rashtra vote on important legislative and judicial issues themselves, and Baaba-Ji executes our decisions. Simple. No more representative middlemen, no more corruption, no more allegations of fascism. One hundred per cent pure democracy only.

'Now, let's turn to today's Poll.'

The wall-TV divided itself into two parts. On the right, the studio remained as it was, but the left side showed a mugshot of a man in a white shirt with a long beard and no moustache. A white skull cap sat like inescapable destiny on his head. 'Undesirable No. 35000071' read the caption underneath the picture.

The Voice was grave when it spoke again. 'As proud citizens of the Rashtra, today you will decide the fate of this animal, this Undesirable, who feeds himself on our soil and eats away at our values and culture like a termite. A goddamn termite. You, and you alone, will decide whether this snake deserves to be put down or thrown out of the Rashtra, free to spread his poison elsewhere. We will take a small break now and get back to you with the details of his crime.'

The studio and the Undesirable dissolved together in a stream of colourful advertisements. Soldiers marched on the screen wearing the 'best knickers in the world,' and little kids brushed their teeth with the 'most effective toothpaste in the known universe.'

'Mute Television,' Papa said, and an abrupt silence took over the room. 'He looks a lot like Abdul.'

Mother and the boys looked at him with uncomprehending eyes.

'He was our milkman when I was married to— I mean, before you all came along. He was as crooked as they all are. Used to make us drink more water than milk.'

Mother chuckled politely. 'This one also looks like a crook, doesn't he? Anyway, I don't understand why all these Undesirables stay so dirty. Are they allergic to soap and water, or what?'

'I wouldn't be surprised if they are. How do you think we should vote, then? Children! Be quiet.'

Sooraj and Anuj, who were squabbling over a small toy car, turned silently to watch the advertisements.

'We know they are all rapists and murderers, don't we?' Mummy replied eagerly with a rhetorical question. She knew how much Papa liked to talk about the horrible ways the Undesirables raped Hindu women before and during the war. It never failed to light up his eyes.

The news studio came back on the wall-TV just as Papa opened his mouth to reply.

'I hope you have had some time to discuss your votes,' the Voice said. 'Now, let me tell you the charges against this termite.

'Undesirable No. 35000071 here has been unemployed for the last fifteen years, and since then, he has been living off the charity of his friends and the infrastructure of our Rashtra, which is paid for by you, the honest taxpayers.

'Now, two months ago, 35000071 decided that the education system designed by our Baaba-Ji was not enough for the children in his neighbourhood.' The Voice's pitch rose steadily. 'This man— this... this absolute cretin thought he had the right to fill the innocent minds of our children with the works of bastards like Rabindranath Tagore and Arundhati Roy. All those poor children are Idea-Infected now.'

Mummy gasped. Everybody knew that reading a prohibited book was punishable by death, and this shameless man had been making little children do that.

The Voice continued, 'He was caught red-handed when one of the parents got wind of what was going on and reported him to the Swayamsevaks at a nearby Shakha. He has admitted to all charges against himself and has shown no remorse for his heinous crimes, we are told by the Swayamsevaks. So, I ask you, does a man like this deserve to live? Does he deserve to be left free to infect other children with his Undesirable thoughts? Can you imagine what else he might have done with those children? Let me tell you, there were girls in his class too, and Brahmin children were found sitting right next to his kitchen.

'Your choices today are simple: do you want to give this man, who is obviously a threat to all of us and our society, a quick and merciful end, or do you throw him out of our Rashtra to be someone else's problem? Vote wisely, I implore you.

'Execution or Exile. The nation wants to know your choice ASAP.'

Darkness descended on the screen, and familiar words flashed across it.

```
For Execution SMS OPTION A <<Your
Aadhaar ID>> to 878787
    For Exile SMS OPTION B <<Your
Aadhaar ID>> to 878787
    The    People's    Poll    is    now
concluded. The results will come to
your TVs tomorrow at 7 p.m. Stay
tuned.
```

Papa took another bite of his roti and sighed. 'The dinner is cold,' he said.

'I'm sorry, let me reheat it. Will only take two minutes. Or I can cook something fresh?'

'No, no. Let it be. But tell me, how do you want to vote?' Papa asked.

'I just know that I didn't like looking at that man. It's not like last week, right? That girl didn't look so bad, and she was still one of us at the end of the day. What will happen to all those children this man taught, do you think? I just can't stop thinking about Anuj and Sooraj meeting such a person and getting Idea-Infected. Anyway, vote however you think best. I'll get your food ready, and then I have a few other chores to finish before we go to bed.'

'You're right, you're right. We did vote for the girl's exile last month. And anyway, Gupta was telling me in the office today that they are keeping a record of our votes to decide our loyalty to the Rashtra and Baaba-Ji. Can't afford to look too soft towards the Undesirables if we want our Aadhaar Score to stay high, can we?'

'Well, there you have it then. Sooraj, give Papa your phone.'

Papa took the two phones offered to him and picked up his own from the table.

'OPTION A 2504xxxx19814,' he typed and sent the message. It felt nothing like passing a death sentence on a stranger.

Mummy took his dinner from him and went to the kitchen to reheat it.

The boys resumed their quarrel over the toy car.

Papa placed his feet up on the table and opened The Good Times of India once again.

A.M. GAUTAM

A.M. Gautam is an internationally published writer from India whose work usually focuses on our zeitgeist through the lens of speculative fiction. His debut essay collection is forthcoming from the *Aleph Book Company* in 2024.

ABOUT THE PUBLISHER

A Coup of Owls Press was formed in early 2021 before publishing our first issue in June 2021. Initially bi-monthly, we now publish a quarterly online issue of eclectic and diverse short fiction that is free to read online or download. We only publish creators from underrepresented and/or marginalised communities or backgrounds. We are a Coup rather than a Parliament. We always strive to embrace the other and the different.

Other & Different is our first print anthology.

www.acoupofowls.com

Dedicated to all the *Other*

& **DIFFERENT**

A Coup Of Owls Press

Ingram Content Group UK Ltd.
Milton Keynes UK
UKHW021815090623
423193UK00013B/833